THE LAST MUTATION

AND OTHER STORIES FROM THE WASTELANDS

MICHAEL BRAY

SEVERED PRESS
HOBART TASMANIA

THE LAST MUTATION

Copyright © 2016 Michael Bray
Copyright © 2016 by Severed Press

WWW.SEVEREDPRESS.COM

ISBN: 978-1-925493-21-4

CHAPTER ONE

This world was death. Once called earth, it was now an inhospitable, rocky place filled with death and the remnants of the old world. The colours of what once went before had become faded, greens and blues replaced by brown and grey. Trees, once lush and alive were now brittle skeletal things whose leaves would never again grow. This wasn't new, or unexpected. Nothing in this world lived, not in the sense of the word as they once did. Instead, humanity survived, those who were left scurrying like cockroaches in an effort to prolong their pitiful existence. A man shambled through these desolate lands, breath fogging in the chill air, scruffy hair and beard tousled by the icy wind. He pulled his tatty green jacket up around his neck in a half-hearted attempt to keep warm, and went on his way, heading nowhere, letting instinct guide him. Nobody counted days or seasons anymore. There was no point. In the old world, it would have been February. In this one, it was simply another bleak and bitter day like the rest. He squinted at the sky, grey and overcast as it always was and always had been for as long as he could remember. He heard that once it used to be blue, but like the sun, now only a hazy whitish glow in the sky, it had become the stuff of legend, a campfire story told by people who were either clinging to what was there before, or looking for renewed hope for the future. The man stopped, tired eyes scanning the landscape. Shells of buildings, broken and forgotten reached up from the ground, tombstones to a society nobody could remember. With them, the rusted shells of cars that snaked through the broken streets, all that remained of the thriving lands that used to exist before the event occurred. He had been born afterwards, when the world was dark and cold, and most of the

1

people of the planet were already dead or dying.

The Event.

That's what they called it, a thing of legend, the event that happened without warning and changed the lives of everyone the world over. The man had heard stories about it, explanations from people who were still struggling to come to terms with it. There were, at least, six different versions, and to the man, none of them seemed any more plausible that the next. For him, in a way, it was easier. He was thirty and had only ever known this world as it was now. He had no knowledge of what came before, of how life used to be, just stories, things left behind for people like him to find, things that were relics of a time gone by. To him, they were just shapes, things passed on the road which had no end, no destination, and no goal. He walked because there was nothing else to do. He walked to survive. Some, he knew, walked in hope, determined to believe there was a better place, that there was somewhere else where life was how it used to be. Some, he knew walked to hunt, even the destruction of the world had left some bad seeds behind. There were stories about these people too, flesh eaters, vile animals who thrived in the place the world had become. The man adjusted his backpack, the tattered green canvas sack containing everything he possessed. Like him, it was falling apart and had been repaired numerous times. He suspected that one day, it, like him would break down altogether. Until that day came, though, he would go on. He would walk these roads and try to find purpose. He had seen things, horrific things that he wanted to forget. He had seen poverty, he had seen pain and he had seen cruelty. The man paused, listening. Dirt rolled across the road, pushed by the acrid, sulphur smelling wind, then settled.

Silence.

This world's heart no longer had a beat. It was dead and desolate, broken and without any hope of salvation. It existed only for the unlucky ones like him who didn't die during the event, and who existed only it to eke out another day of purposeless survival, shuffling around like broken ghouls with nothing left to haunt but their own fractured psyches. An old man once told him that there used to be more than four billion people living in this hellish place. That number was impossible for him to comprehend. He estimated he had encountered fewer than a hundred people during his lifetime. To imagine four billion people once existing was something he couldn't begin to imagine. He walked on, the sole of his right boot hanging loose at the toe and flopping against the cracked tarmac with every step. The left was holding up well. The boots weren't a matching pair, and like everything, had been collected on the road. He had scavenged the left one from a dead man, his rotten, withered corpse face down in a ditch. He didn't know what had happened to him, but there had only been one leg on the body when he found it. The dead man was the same size foot, and the boot was of good quality, so he took it. This was what life had become. Scavenging from the dead, picking around the remains of the world to survive. Finding a boot to replace the broken one was on his mind. Without boots he couldn't walk, if he couldn't walk, he couldn't find food, if he couldn't find food, he would die. The mechanics were simple. Keep walking, keep surviving. He walked down the centre of the road, the sound of his broken shoe the only break in the silence.

Slap.

Slap.

Slap.

His hands were going numb from the cold, and he put them into the pockets of his jacket. His beard ruffled, bringing another stench of that awful, burnt-match smell that lingered on the air and had done since the event. He had entered what was once a city, steel shells of buildings with broken windows towering around him. Some had collapsed, others were sagging, and others were in remarkably good condition. He knew better than to go into them. Those were the kinds of places the flesh eaters hid from the day, waiting for unsuspecting travellers to go in search of supplies. He had heard stories of people being trapped in such buildings, and although he needed new footwear, he wasn't about to risk his life to get it. Instead, he walked on, eyes scanning, always looking for the next opportunity to scavenge. He walked the streets of the city, picking through rubbish when it was in the open and safe to do so, avoiding places where traps may be waiting. It was hard work and such long periods of focus and concentration were exhausting. He paused to rest, entering what used to be a coffee shop. The plate glass windows were broken, the interior of the shop filled with a thick layer of dust. There was no plant life. Everything organic had died in the days following the event. He stepped over the threshold of the coffee shop, leaving footprints in the dust like he was the first visitor to a new planet. He picked up an overturned chair which was lying on its side and sat, the tired wood creaking under him. Positioning himself so he was both out of sight but could see down the street if anyone should come. The man set his bag down between his feet, opened it and looking inside. These were his things, his prized possessions, everything he owned in the world. These were the things he had collected on the road, memories of strangers, of lives he had never known or experienced. It was his window to the past, to a world he had never known. It was his way of trying to figure out what had happened and what his place in the world was. They were windows into a time he would never know, a time before newspapers no longer existed to report on world events, when people stopped killing and bickering over petty things such as land and resources and turned their attention towards survival in a barren new world. He treasured these things, these windows into a time before his own. Each one was a special memory, and each had a unique feel to him. He took some of them out now from the tin he kept in the bottom of his bag, his hands gentle and caring as they sifted through the letters, the notes, the lives of other people reduced to nothing but a few tattered and crumbling pages. Somehow, he felt attached to these people, these anonymous strangers he would never meet and who were probably dead. He took the creased postcard from the top of the pile, the edges frayed, the picture faded. He ran his fingers over the image, unable to imagine such a place could have once existed. It was a beach. Golden sands and blue skies. Taken from above, the beach was filled with people on sun loungers or frolicking in the surf. All of them were dead now, of course, there was no doubt of that. Or were they? He paused to consider the question. Could it be that he had perhaps passed one of the people from this picture on the road during his endless journey? Could they have been one of the filthy, haunted ghosts he had met coming in the opposite direction, people who like him were trying to find a place, a purpose, a direction. Perhaps they held on to the memories of sitting there on that beach, basking in the sun with nothing to worry about but making sure they didn't over tan. His dirty fingers brushed over the ocean, tracing the frothy white line where the water touched the sand. He couldn't imagine what such a place would look like. He didn't know how to get there, or if it even still existed. The ocean, a place he dreamed about seeing but didn't know if he ever would. He supposed that if he went in a straight line in any one direction for long enough, he would reach it. Sadly, the world didn't work that way. He went where instinct told him, to the places where he knew he could scavenge out another day of existence. He turned the card over. Someone had written in it, the black ink faded but still legible, the words long committed to his memory.

Greetings from the sun!

Mary and I were just about to go for cocktails and thought we better send this home to you in the rain. I hope the kids are behaving for you; if not, tell them we'll hold back their pocket money! We'll see you in three weeks.

Best,

David

He put the postcard on the bottom of the pile and picked up the letter beneath it. Like many of the memories he had collected, it was a tragic snapshot of the world of the past. He carefully unfolded the faded yellow paper and let his eyes drift over the words.

Dear Julia,

I know you will never read this, as you haven't yet been born, which is something I'm grateful for, as much as I hate myself for it. I know writing this to you makes no sense, but I need to explain my actions and why I have to do what I'm about to do. We haven't eaten for days now, and I fear for you. Although some say I'm lucky to carry new life inside me, that I'm the future of the human race, the truth is that I don't want to be responsible for bringing you into what is left of the world. It's an awful, awful place now and not a day goes by when I don't wish we had been killed during the event. Last week, I met another survivor, someone who claimed to have fished the shore by the coast. He said the ocean there bubbled and burned, spewing lava like the pit of hell, the water hot as it came in with the tides and melted the sand, turning it to black glass. I don't know if it's true. To me, it sounds impossible, but the idea that it might be means I can't bring you into this world. I just can't. There were other things he said, things even more frightening than the lack of future I see for us. He told me there were things in the water – mutants – things that used to be animals but had changed. According to him, another group had been attacked by one as they had tried to fish offshore and all but one were killed.

I was desperate not to believe him, but I could see from the look in his eyes that he was telling the truth. How can I bring you into this world knowing that, at best, your future will be one of scratching around and trying to survive? I wish there were some kind of hope to give you, but there is none. None at all.

Everyone we once knew is gone, and there is nobody here to help us. That's not the life I want for you. Or for me. I tried to think of the most humane way to do this, and although I would have preferred something quick like a gun, I wouldn't have the first clue where to find one. There is a bridge near here which is broken but still stands, and although I had considered it, I don't want you to be in the water and be eaten by one of those god-awful things, or captured by raiders and sold for meat. That idea terrifies me. I wish I were older or wiser, or even still had my mother to ask for advice, but like so many people, she died during the event. I miss her, I miss them both. It's cruel that I lived when everyone else we knew died. So, so cruel. Because of that, and the fact that I truly believe there is no hope left in the world, I have decided that hanging would be best for us. Only I will feel the pain, and I suppose I deserve it. You, my angel, will never know what has happened, or will never have to endure this horrible place. That brings me comfort.

Please don't see this as a rash decision. I have done nothing but think about it since the idea came to me. In the end, it comes down to quality of life. I would rather we went out this way than wait to die slowly. I found us a nice quiet place in the woods not far from here. The trees there are dead and burned, but I found one that is big and still strong enough to hold the rope. At least this way, there will be no pain and we will see each other again in the afterlife if there is one. I have to hope and pray that there is and that if God is real, he forgives me for what I'm about to do.

Please forgive me, my angel.

Know that I had no other choice.
July 10th

#

He had found the Julia letter in a backpack near a forest. He didn't go any deeper into the woods; he had no desire to see if the words penned had come to fruition, but even now, years after finding it, he wondered who Julia was, what she looked like, if she went through with it or changed her mind. He hoped for the latter but suspected the former. The world was an awful place, and he couldn't imagine how it must be to face the idea of bringing a child up in it. He went back to the postcard, staring at the image. He had found it almost three years earlier on the street, just lying there in the dirt outside a crumbling home as if waiting for him, a splash of colour in a bleak and faded world. No matter how often he looked at it, he was still mesmerised by the image. In his world of brown and grey, he couldn't imagine such vibrancy could exist.

#

He had found some new boots. A department store had at one point in the past been looted, and clothes and products were strewn all over the road and forgotten. Many of the clothes were rotten from exposure to the elements, racks of shirts and jeans now nothing more than stinking mould-covered piles which were almost unidentifiable and coated in a thick green and black skin. He knew this mould was potentially lethal. He had heard stories of people trying to eat it, due to the worldwide shortage of food, and growing ill, some even dying as the toxins ravaged their body. He suspected that was why the scatter of goods still remained. Most, he assumed, would have ignored it; however, he knew that as long as he didn't inhale or ingest it, he would be fine. He made a basic face mask from his scarf and started to dig down into the pile of old shirts and jeans, the lower layers damp and stinking, but at least they were mould free. The boots were still in their box and in reasonable shape. There were a dozen boxes of them towards the bottom of the pile. Some were no good, either too small or the wrong type of footwear for wasteland survival, but one pair at least were useable. They were good sturdy boots, and although they were a little too big, they were much better than the ones he had been wearing. He put them on, thrilled with his find and relieved to finally be throwing away his worn-down old pair that was close to falling off his feet from overuse. The new ones felt odd, but he was sure they would break in eventually. He wiped his hands on his jeans, getting as much of the black mould off him and then turned his attention back towards his next move. Darkness was starting to draw in and a bitter, sulphur-smelling rain was starting to fall. Knowing how vital it was to stay warm and dry – hypothermia or pneumonia would be a death sentence for anyone exposed to the elements for too long – he had chosen to wait it out in a medium-sized home on the outskirts of the city. It was a calculated risk; raiders were less likely to use such a place to ambush unsuspecting travellers, instead preferring the bigger buildings with networks of rooms and corridors. Even so, he observed the home from outside for some time, watching from across the street, looking for movement behind the filthy, dust-covered windows. Trusting his instincts that it was safe, he crossed the street and opened the gate. A red child's bicycle lay on its side in the yard, its frame rusted away, its tires rotten, and its owner now likely long dead along with everyone else. The man ignored it and approached the house. The door was warped, its paint brittle and flaking. He could imagine the house as one that was nice in the old world. He looked down the street at the other dozen homes, wondering how it must be under blue skies with trees and grass. Now just the shells remained. He tried the door handle, but it was locked. This, he had learned, was no longer an issue. Age had become his ally. He put his shoulder to the door on the edge where the lock would be housed and shoved. The tired wood splintered and gave way, the door creaking open and leaving the handle and lock still in place. Beyond, the hall carpet was dry and coated in dust, the photographs on the walls the same. He saw this as a good sign. If other people had been in the house, there would be footprints, signs of looting. Instead, it was like looking into a time capsule. Wallpaper had come away from the walls and lay in curled piles on the floor. Dusty coats hung on a peg rack in the hall that the owners would never again wear. He stepped into the house and closed the door, realigning the wood around the broken lock as best he could. With luck, anyone passing would not notice it had been disturbed. Satisfied that the repair job was as good as it was going to get, he walked deeper into the house, little puffs of dust displaced with each footstep. Outside, a spectacular thunderstorm had broken the silence, the rain now driving down with fury. He was glad to be inside. He walked around the house, checking every room, making sure he was alone. It looked like it had, at one point, been a family home, which made its utter abandonment seem all the sadder. He checked the coat rack and found a blue rain jacket, which was better than the one he was wearing. There was no hesitation. He dusted it down and put it on, leaving his old tattered green jacket hanging in its place. The downstairs housed a kitchen, the cupboards completely empty, and the fridge stinking and mouldy. An old newspaper was on the table, but it was directly underneath a leak in the roof and was impossible to open without turning to mush. Upstairs were three bedrooms. One was bare and without carpets, the other looked like a master bedroom, or at least it had been. The double bed and the walls were covered in the same black mould as the pile of clothes where he had found the boots. The man stood on the threshold of the room and saw the reason why. A gaping hole in the ceiling was letting in the rain and he suspected was the source of the leak in the kitchen. He closed the door, knowing that taking a risk to get new boots was fine, risking exploring this room when he didn't need to was tempting fate. The third room was a child's room. The walls had been painted in blues with a mural of a castle and soldiers with huge smiling faces. The paint was faded, but he could imagine how good it would have looked when it was fresh. A broken cabin bed lay against one wall, the mattress missing. He thought of the bike out in the front yard and was already starting to paint a picture of the people who once lived there. Downstairs, there was a bathroom which as unremarkable and empty, and a sitting room which, like everything else was covered with a thick layer of dust. This room had so far not been touched by the damp and looked mostly intact. Outside, the thunderstorm raged as the clouds illuminated in spectacular fashion, lightning bolt after lightning bolt thrown in rapid succession from the sky. Some people said storms were never like this before the event, but like everything else, it was just a story, something people said. Something in the room caught his eye. There was a notebook on the table, a large rock balanced on top of it to hold it in place. He crossed the room and moved the rock, then picked up the book. It was very old and fragile, the paper brittle and yellow, the handwriting scrawled and desperate. The man returned to the sofa, brushing away the dust as best he could manage, then lying down and putting his feet up. For a while, he watched the light show as the thunder raged outside, then tiring of watching, he opened the notepad to the first page. This was what he did, this was how he survived in the world. He collected memories, snapshots from other lives. He had no name of his own, and so when people would ask, he just told them he was the Collector. It was as fitting a title as any for what he did. Making himself comfortable, he started to read

INTERLUDE ONE
Billy, Malorie and the Shelter

It seemed like Billy had been waiting for that siren to go off all his life, or at least for the last five years of it. He always told me it would be coming, he was always so sure. The end of the world, the apocalypse. End of days. He was always so serious about it. He spent five years ignoring the sniggers, the pointing and the stares of all those people who said he was crazy. Even I thought it of him, his own wife, isn't that awful? Even so, despite it all, Billy had the last laugh, because he was right. When that flash of light illuminated the air and that siren fired up, so shrill and piercing, those people who pointed and laughed (me included) didn't know what to do. Billy did though, and within five minutes, he and I were in the bunker under the house, the one he had sweated over to afford and install to a backdrop of sniggers. We spent that first few nights listening to the dull sound explosions and screams coming from the surface and could only speculate on what was going on. There was no television, no internet, and no phone line. Everything was offline. All we had was each other, those steel-walled rooms and enough supplies to live comfortably for three years. The shelter even had its own power generator and air-filtration system. Billy had done well with it, although under the circumstances, there was little to celebrate, not for me at least. I'm not sure what was going through Billy's mind though, because as we sat there in the dark, listening to those horrific sounds from above ground, he couldn't stop smiling. He kept repeating that he was right, how he knew the day would come when all his work would pay off. I can't argue with him, or blame him. Thanks to his dedication (some would say paranoid fantasy), we were alive during whatever was going on topside. We don't know what's going on up there, but we know it's big, a major event. For three hours, we tried to find a radio frequency to listen in on, but there was nothing, just a band full of static punctuated by dead silence when we found a station. Billy said it must be big trouble, because although the stations were there where they should be, the airwaves were dead. Billy joked that maybe the presenters were too. I didn't find it funny, but he did. He laughed it up, his voice echoing around the metal walls in a way that it no longer sounded like laughter. In that moment, I think I was more scared of him than whatever was happening on the surface.

DAY THREE

There had been no noise from above ground for two full days now. Somehow, the silence is worse. Billy is still trying daily to get a radio signal, even though it's clear by now that there is nothing out there for us to pick up. That's frightening. It makes me wonder if it's fate or misfortune that brought me to this point. As I sit here on the cold wood bench, curved steel at my back and heavy silence above, I watch him stalk around the shelter, counting bottles of water, double and triple checking our supplies. It comes to me that he is happy, really happy for the first time in years. The death of the world seems to have come at the perfect time for him. To his credit, we have plenty down here to keep us going. I asked him just now when we might be able to return to the surface and help people, and he gave me that look, that cocky half-sneer that I've grown to hate. He told me the supplies were for us and not for them, and it was unsafe to go to the surface. He said he wondered who was laughing at him now. I asked him how he could possibly know how safe or unsafe it was up there when we are so cut off from the world. Billy shrugged and said it was probably nuclear war. Probably the Russians, maybe one of the terror groups had managed to get their hands on some kind of device. ISIS, he speculates.

That seems unlikely, especially as whatever has happened

seems to have reached far and wide. Then there was that flash in the sky just before the siren. If it were a bomb, surely an explosion would have accompanied that sound, but that didn't happen. Just light and silence and the smell of burnt matches. I want to reason with him and explain my thoughts on this, but don't want to get into an argument, not here, not in a place that is clearly his domain, his territory. Billy has already made it perfectly clear that I'm a guest here, just another possession to go with the canned goods and water supplies. Part of me wonders if I'm on his checklist too.

DAY FIVE

Time works differently down here. Before the event, it was easy to exist alongside Billy because we had other distractions around us. Television, friends, things to ensure we didn't have to interact with each other too much. With all that stuff gone, it makes me realise how little we have in common. Sharing this space with him is becoming unbearable. He's started ranting, muttering to himself about how he was chosen to survive, how he'd heard a message from God telling him to make plans to live. He asked me if I knew how lucky I was to be included in his plan, and likened himself to Noah before the great flood. I nodded and agreed with him. I was too afraid not to.

The irony is, that I was ready to leave him, in fact I was all set to leave him the day it happened. For too long, I've had to suffer his pompous, self-absorbed ranting. He's old school, one of those people who believe men go to work and women stay at home in the kitchen. Even down here, that trend has continued. I'm expected to make all the meals, even though he's there anyway standing over my shoulder, telling me to make sure I don't use too much, that we have to make it last. How I'd love to tell him to do it himself if he thinks he can do better, but I can't do that. He's made it clear that this is his place, his show, and he is in charge. I'm not sure he'd throw me out, only because I don't think he'd risk opening the shelter hatch yet, but he's cruel enough to do something to punish me. Maybe deny me some food or water or something, just a gesture to show that he's the boss. So, as frustrating as it is, it's easier to take it, just like I used to before the event. Like it was when we lived up on the surface. I put up with the ranting, the frustration, the fear and the silence on my own, soaking it up like a sponge. I realise there is no love between us. Not anymore. I feel cold to him, resentful. Of all the people who shouldn't have been proved right, it was him. It changed him, made him arrogant and cocky. Now he thinks he's something he's not. He has some kind of weird god complex which is a concern. He's expecting me to go to bed with him now, I can hear him calling me, saying he has needs to fulfil. The thought of him touching me, pawing at me as he climbs on top makes me feel sick. Like the rest of it, there is no love in the physical act. He's as selfish there as he is everywhere else, pleasing only himself. I told him I'm concerned about pregnancy, especially now with the world the way it is. Could you imagine bringing up a child in a world like this? How irresponsible would that be? Billy though, like always, has the answer. He says he has protection, plenty to last as long as we could ever need (oh joy). It looks like I will have to get used to the idea that he's going to have his way regardless of anything else and I'll have to just do my best to cope with it.

DAY TWELVE

This is unbearable.

Billy barely speaks anymore. He sits in the corner, nose buried in his Bible. It's ironic, as he was never religious and always said he never believed in anything apart from the value of the

American dollar, but now he seems to have had a change of heart. Every now and again, he will look up at me, eyes as wide as his grin and recite a passage to me. God he looks a mess. He hasn't washed or shaved since we came down here. He looks awful, smells worse. I have to nod and agree with him as always, not because I'm trying to keep him sweet anymore, but because I'm scared of him. Even though the Billy from before was starting to seem distant to me, this version of him is a total stranger. For the first time, I'm starting to wish I was out of the house when the event happened so that he couldn't have brought me down here. I know that might sound selfish, but I can't help it. I don't think it would have bothered Billy. He'd have come down to the shelter without a second thought for me, that much is obvious. It's getting to the point where I think I'd rather have died up there than have to spend any more time listening to him rant, or lie there in that bunk as he pumps away on top of me, eyes glassy and staring at the wall so he doesn't have to look at me until he's done. It got me to thinking about the people I left behind. My parents, my sister, my friends. I resent him for it, for dragging me down here into this place. Any sense of connection to the outside world is starting to fade, and not for the first time I ask myself if this is really living, or just existing. I wonder what it's like up there on the surface, then soon enough find myself having to shut those thoughts off because the answers to the questions might frighten me more than I am already if that's at all possible. This life is hell.

DAY FOURTEEN

I hate him. He hasn't slept for two solid days now. All he does is read that Bible. He's started to take notes, and the walls of the shelter are starting to fill up with yellow sticky notes with verses and passages scrawled onto them. Yesterday, as we ate our rice and beans, he told me we needed to start thinking about the future, about our long-term plan. I considered asking him why he was even consulting me about it when he will do what he wants to do regardless, but didn't want another argument, so I played nice and asked him what he meant. He said it was clear enough that the world was dead (how he reached this conclusion I don't know; since we came down here, we have been completely isolated), and we now have to think about repopulating for future generations. That was a worry, and I asked him what he meant. He told me he wanted to start thinking about us having more children, starting off a new bloodline. That was too much, and I lost it. I told him it was irresponsible, and that thinking about bringing children into the world was crazy. I was sure I'd pushed him too far. He got this look in his eye, rage and defiance, anger and a little bit of madness. He asked me who I was to think I could question his decisions, and that he would do what was in the best interests of the world in order to ensure the human race survived. I told him I wouldn't be a part of it, and he swiped the food off the table, plastic dishes spilling lukewarm food all over the floor. He asked me why I thought I had a choice, and reminded me that I was only there because he chose to let me live.

I countered by asking him why he thought he was some kind of god. He said he was more than a god. That was a worry, and stopped me in my tracks. He said he had been given divine knowledge of the end of times and been given the opportunity to prepare for it. He said he had spoken to God, and had been told that the world was soon to be a blank canvas for him to reshape in the way it should have been. He grabbed me then, hard fingers digging into my arms, his face inches from mine. He told me the world of old was a bad place, filled with corruption and greed. He said he and I could change it, be the mother and father of the new world because we had been chosen to do so by a higher power. He said our bloodline would be pure, how our children would mate with their siblings so that, in time, the planet would be filled with variations of ourselves. I screamed at him and told him I wouldn't do it, I'd have no part of it. That was when he hit me. Not a slap, but a balled fist to the face. The explosion of heat and pain was only marginally worse than the shock. He stood over me, defiant and angry and said I would either learn to do things his way or he would make things difficult for me. Later that night, he took me. He came to the bunk I was lying in and pretending to be asleep and climbed on me. He didn't use any protection, and I was too weak-willed to stop him. When he finished and released his warmth into me, he whispered in my ear that he loved me.

I wanted to scream.

DAY THIRTY-SIX

I'm scared.

Really scared, so much so that I'm considering leaving and trying my luck on the surface. Since the day he hit me at the dinner table, things have fallen into a pattern. We wake, I cook, and Billy reads his Bible. I clean and wash up, Billy takes inventory and reads more of that damn book, and then he takes me when it suits him. The act itself has become robotic. He won't even face me anymore, he just bends me over whatever is close and goes at it, grunting at me that it's all about the survival of the human race. I'm a toy to him, a slave. A vessel for his insane plan to become some kind of father to the whole planet. That's what I think has happened to him. Insanity, madness. I think there may have been a little of it before, maybe some undiagnosed condition that I shrugged off as weirdness during the whole prepping thing before the event. Now though, I'm pretty sure there is something seriously wrong with him. Every few days, he makes me take a pregnancy test, and every time it's negative, I feel relief inside then pain as he tells me there 'must be something wrong with my plumbing,' and that he's disappointed in me. After that, he usually beats me as punishment for 'letting the human race down.' Bastard. I fucking hate him, hate him more than anything. The idea of being stuck here with him for who knows how long terrifies me. It's not like I can just get him to see a doctor or get some medication. It's just the two of us down here and only a matter of time before he makes me pregnant. Last night, I woke up and could hear him talking. I got out of my bunk and crept through to the main shelter room. This is the central hub almost. Most of our food is in here along with the radio equipment. Billy was sitting there at the radio console talking. At first, I thought he had managed to get through to someone and that the nightmare might be over, but as I watched, I realised there was just static coming through, not that Billy noticed. He was having a full conversation with himself, talking about repopulating and doing what was right. I stayed there in the shadows, watching him for a while, wondering what had happened to him, then went to bed before he noticed I was there. Some things are just too difficult to explain, and I think that would be one of them. At least things can't get much worse than this, can they?

DAY THIRTY-NINE

I'm pregnant.

I did two tests and both are positive. Billy is elated, and still manages to get in a little jibe about how it's a good job the plumbing started to work as he was pretty sure I was broken.

Bastard.

I hate myself for letting this happen. I dread to think what it might be like up there on the surface, and how it must be so much worse than what I'm going through, which in turn makes me feel guilty for feeling so bad. I try to convince myself that it might not be too bad up there, and we had badly overreacted by coming down here, but then I realise the lack of radio or television reception is a very bad sign and tells me that things are only going to get worse. Plus, there was the bright light, and the screams and the explosions. Even so, I have been thinking about leaving again, only this time I'm serious. I could go when Billy is asleep and take a few supplies with me. After all, it was my money as well as his that paid for all this stuff. I'm entitled. My main concerns are actually getting out of here (the hatch is twenty feet up a ladder) without him hearing me. The thought of what he might do to me if he catches me trying to escape with his precious supplies, especially now that I'm carrying his child, is too terrifying to consider. My other worry is what might be waiting for me up there. What if I do everything I set out to, if I steal the supplies, manage to escape and get free, only to find out there's nothing left and he was right all along? I don't think I could handle that. I really need to think about this and keep him sweet until I make a decision. God only knows what he would do to me if he found out.

DAY FORTY-SIX

I have a plan. I would have liked more time to think things through, but I'm not prepared to stay here any longer. I think he knows I'm up to something, and I need to act fast before he finds out. Jesus, this diary alone would be enough to make him go crazy and do something bad. First things first though, I need to write down what happened yesterday if only to see it on paper and convince myself it was the right thing to do.

Billy made a list, he called it his family tree. He was so proud as he stood there beside me to show me it, and it took all me efforts not to shrink away from his touch or scream when I saw it.

His name was at the top (no sign of mine on there even though I'm the one carrying the child) and below it, branching off were names of the children he planned to have, each of them paired off together, boy and girl, the names of their children below them. He had given them all biblical names lifted from his favourite book. I asked him how he could guarantee there would be more children, and even if they were, there was no guarantee on the sex. He had an answer to that one too. He said there would have to be a little bit of population control. I half suspected what he meant by that, but he elaborated and left little doubt. He said if we happened to have too many of any one particular sex, they would have to be culled on birth to ensure a good balance. He said it like he was referring to some kind of animal, not a child, not another human. He then said I should be good for maybe the first eight or nine children before I would be too old and he would have to start looking for a replacement. He said this with such calm assurance that I was almost able to accept it. He said he didn't like to have to do it, but we all had to make sacrifices in order to make sure the human race continued. I nodded and told him I understood, even though I didn't. None of it made any sense, none of it would sink in and stay in my mind. All I can do is keep thinking about escape, getting out of here. It's going to have to be soon. I know now that nothing up there could be worse than what's happening down here.

Which, incidentally, brings me to my plan. I think I have a way to do it, although the more I think about it becoming a reality, the more afraid I get. I stole some sleeping pills from the medical supplies. Tonight, when Billy is up and talking to the static on the radio, I plan to crush them up into a powder. Tomorrow morning when I make breakfast, I'm going to mix it into his food. I was uncertain how much to give him. The package says no more than four to be taken every twenty-four hours, but I really want to knock him out so I intend to crush up six. That should give me enough time to get some supplies together and get out before he wakes up. I'm pretty sure he would be too afraid to follow me out of here. This shelter is his life, the one thing he loves and cares about. Besides, even if he did follow me, he wouldn't know where I'd gone. The truth is, I don't know where I'd go either. Whatever is going on up there is a mystery to me. We've been down here for well over a month, and apart from the chaos of those first few days, there has been no noise of any kind. I feel so sick, so scared, but I have to do this. I can't stay here with him, not anymore. The things he has planned are frightening and disgusting. Taking my chances on the surface seems to be my only option. I only hope things go smoothly.

DAY FORTY-SEVEN

Billy's dead.

I've been sitting here trembling in the bunker for the last three hours and didn't know what else to do but write in this book. It has been my one constant, my friend, my companion. As I sit here, I can see him on the floor. He's surrounded by plastic dishes and food, his white T-shirt almost fully saturated with blood. The handle of the carving knife is still sticking up out of his chest. I keep looking at him and expecting him to stand up and scream at me that it was all a joke, but his eyes have been open and staring at the roof since it happened, so I think I can be safe to assume he's definitely dead. This isn't what I wanted, this isn't how I planned it to be. I have blood on me. God, it's everywhere. On the floor, on the walls, on the table. On me and this book I'm writing in. There was so much of it. I feel sick, and yet strangely relieved. He was broken, damaged beyond repair. The man I one loved died on the surface long ago without me realising. This monster I have been trapped with is – was – a stranger to me. I'll be leaving soon, but first, I need to tell what happened, if only to try and justify what I did to him. I'll be taking this diary with me and leaving it somewhere safe. At least it might give me a little closure and help me to move on. It will be a symbolic gesture, leaving behind the last memory of the worst time I can recall as soon as I feel safe enough to move on alone. First though, an explanation.

One thing I never accounted for in my plan was Billy's meticulous inventory taking. It was an oversight, a mistake. The truth is, I thought I was outsmarting him, but he was wise to it. He knew the pills had gone, and put the rest together. He'd been watching me, just waiting for me to do exactly what I did. We sat there at the small table, two strangers who had been changed beyond recognition. I set the plate of eggs and beans in front of him and waited for him to start eating so I could put my plan into action before I lost my nerve. Billy didn't start to eat though. He sat there and stared at me, that look in his eye making me fear him in the most unimaginable way. He pushed his plate away and asked me if I thought I was clever, or special. I was screaming inside at this point, but played dumb anyway. He told me he had given me the opportunity to be a part of something special, something beyond the mundane life we had before. I tried to answer, but he swept his arm across the table, sending plates and glasses crashing to the floor. I was too afraid to move, too afraid to do anything other than sit there and watch as he stood up, taking his time, leering at me across the table top. He said he said he wasn't as stupid as I thought he was, he said he knew everything I was thinking, everything I was planning. He said he's read this journal when I was sleeping and was just waiting for me to make my move. Words don't come easy when faced with things like that, so I just sat there and looked at him, unsure what I should even say. He told me I wouldn't be allowed to leave. That I was carrying his property. He said he had tried to do things the easy way but I wasn't to be trusted, and so now things would change. He said he was preparing a room, a place for me to live where he could keep an eye on me. I told him I wouldn't be his prisoner, and he said it wasn't my choice to make, that he didn't see any other way until I learned my place. I panicked at that. I saw visions of a small, dark, windowless room and hours spent alone unless it was time to feed or fuck. I lurched to my feet intending to run, but he was too quick, and was around the table and had a hold of my hair. He pulled me close to him, teeth gritted, nose inches from mine. He told me he'd kill me before he let me leave, and I believed him. It was right there in his eyes. My hands reached for something, anything, knocking pans and cups to the floor from the side of the sink where they were waiting to be washed. My hands found the handle of the knife, and although I'd like to say I took a second to consider the consequences, it would be a lie. I aimed for his chest, for the black heart that drummed inside him. I wasn't sure what to expect, but the knife was razor sharp and went in easy. He didn't scream, or fall down straight away. He held on to me for a while, mouth open, eyes wide and disbelieving. I just watched him, trembling and crying. Those few seconds felt to me like they had lasted a lifetime, then he let go of me and crumpled to the floor.

That's where he is now. Still staring. I know in Victorian times they had a belief that a murder victim's killer was imprinted on their eye after death. I wondered if that was the case with Billy, if I was the last thing he had seen before he shuffled off to meet the god he thought he was so close to. It doesn't matter now. I thought about staying, maybe dumping the body somewhere outside and coming back, but I don't think I could do that. This place is tainted. It's *his* place, and even though he's dead, he will always be here, leering at me.

No. I have to leave. My fate will be at the mercy of whatever is on the surface. I only hope there is something out there to live for.

GOODBYE

This will be my final entry. It will be a shame to leave this journal behind, but I don't think I want it with me anymore. It came from the shelter, and like it or not, it reminds me of Billy, and what I did to him. It's odd that I feel so attached to it. Just thoughts on bound paper, but they were mine and helped me through some rough times. The hardest part of this entire ordeal was getting the courage to open the hatch and climb out into the world. I don't need to tell anyone who finds this what the world is like now, and I wish I had some insight into whatever devastating event has happened and changed the future of humanity forever. The truth is, I probably know less than most. The good news is there are still some good people out here trying to survive. A nice family have taken me in and let me stay for a few days. They have a son, a little boy. They are everything Billy and I were not. They are strong, a unit doing all they can to protect their child. I'm not starting to show yet, but I soon will and then won't be able to deny what I'm carrying around inside me. Part of me is afraid that this child will be like its father and carry his traits, but then I look at the world as it is now and see it in part how he did. Sure enough, something awful has happened, and the suffering will go on for some time yet, but humanity isn't dead yet. Our species are fighters, and incredibly adaptive. One day, when that white light in the sky dims, and that awful smell of burning matches fades away, it will be left to those of us who are left to rebuild. Ironic maybe, that it's a similar idea to the one Billy was trying to push, but I think they are different enough for me to write it down. The fact that there are already survivors of whatever happened is a testament to our strength. I'm going to leave this journal here in the home of these wonderful kind people who have taken me in. Tomorrow, we are all going to go back to the shelter and take all the supplies we can carry then set out to help as many people as we can. I honestly don't know if there is a long-term future for us, but I'm determined to make the best world I can for my unborn child. How far we will get is anyone's guess. But I don't feel like I need to write anymore down. I have people around me who I can talk to, and to lift that weight off my shoulders when I feel close to breaking. They understood what I did to Billy and why I had to do it, which is more than I could have ever hoped for. Mark, the husband of the family I'm staying with, even offered to go down to get the supplies from the shelter, so I don't have to look at Billy's body. I'm grateful for that. If I've learned anything from this whole ordeal, it's strength. I'm stronger now than the woman who first went down into that shelter, and I suppose in a strange way I have Billy to thank for it. I won't thank him though; he doesn't deserve it. Now, I want to focus on looking forward and hoping the future holds something for us, for all of us. I can only hope that it does.

Malorie

CHAPTER TWO

It had been three days since the Collector had eaten. His wanderings had taken him out of the city and into what would once have been countryside. There were no green fields or crops anymore. They had died after the event. Now all that remained was dead, spoiled earth in which nothing could grow. Trees which were once lush with foliage were dried up, dead relics to the past. Many had fallen, some leaned precariously close to joining them. Such things were ordinary to him, and so he paid them no attention. He walked on, hands in the pockets of his blue rain jacket, shoulders bunched against the bitter chill. His stomach growled in need, but the man ignored it. There was nothing he could do right now to satisfy its cravings. He still had water at least. Precious water to keep him alive just a little longer. He had collected it during the rainstorm. It was brown and tasted of ash, but it eased his persistent thirst. He stopped walking, all thoughts of hunger, thirst and the rub of new boots on tired heels forgotten.

There was a man on the road.

He was sitting on the stoop of a partially collapsed church. He was old and completely bald, his dirty skin cracked and pitted like well-worn leather. The two strangers stared at each other, unsure what to do. The man approached, keeping a cautious distance.

"You ain't one of them bad ones, are ye?" the old man said.

The Collector said nothing; he simply stood there and stared.

The old man grinned, his mouth for the most part toothless. "No, it seems you ain't one of them, are you?"

Still, the Collector didn't speak. His instinct told him to run, but part of him was curious. He couldn't remember the last time he saw another human being who actually wanted to talk to him. Most walked by with their heads down and did anything to avoid eye contact. The old man was different. He seemed interested.

"Come on closer, boy. I won't hurt ye. There's been enough hurt in this world as it is."

The Collector moved closer to the man, coming to within ten feet of him, still cautious and ready to run at the first sign of trouble. The old man made no effort to move, he simply sat there, hands folded in his lap. One knee of his grey pants had a hole in it, the bony appendage poking out.

"You look like hell, son. Where ye headed?" the old man said, flashing his toothless grin.

The Collector shrugged.

"You're one o' them drifters, ain't ya? No idea where ye wanna be but nowhere to stay either."

He nodded.

"Come on, son, there must be somewhere ye want to get to?"

The Collector decided there was no immediate danger. The man was both old and alone, and showed no sign of hostility. Maybe he was just interested in the lives of those who passed on the road. He looked far too weak to do much walking of his own. The Collector looked at the half-collapsed church at the old man's back and wondered if this was where he had decided to see out the rest of his days.

"Well, son, you got a tongue in that mouth? Where is it ye wantin' to get to?"

The Collector shrugged off his backpack and rummaged inside. He took out the postcard of the beach and showed it to the old man.

He leaned forward and screwed up his eyes so he could see it, then started to laugh, slapping his leg with the palm of his bony hand.

"What's so funny?" the Collector said.

"Nothin', son, it's just I ain't seen the sea lookin' like that in more than thirty years. Easy to forget it was once blue and not that shitty grey colour it is now."

"You've seen it? The sea, I mean?" the Collector asked.

"Oh yeah. You're not too far away from it right now as it happens, although, it don't look much like that picture anymore."

"Where is it, which way?" the Collector said. All caution in him was gone. He was excited by the possibility of actually seeing the ocean.

"Now you just hang on. It's not as easy as just running off down the road and getting there. Well, it is, but you wouldn't want to right now."

"Why?"

The old man leaned closer, lowering his voice even though there was nobody else around. "Cannibals."

"What does that mean?" the Collector said.

"You don't know about the cannibals?"

"No, what is it?"

"Not an it, it's a *they*. Came through here a couple of days back. I had to hide. Nasty people."

"What's so bad about them?"

"Well, they…" The old man hesitated, then stood, wincing as his tired joints creaked in protest. "Tell you what. You come on inside, and I'll tell you all about it. By the looks of you, you haven't eaten for a few days either."

The Collector looked past the old man to the half-collapsed church, then at the sparse land around them.

"You don't need to be scared of me, boy. I'm just an old man. What I do have is food, shelter and information. Believe me, you'll want that last if you intend to make your way down to the coast."

"Why?"

"Because it ain't like your picture postcard. You go down there, and you need to be aware that there are things in the water that might change your mind. Now are you comin' in or not?"

The old man shuffled into the church, disappearing into the dark and shadow-draped building. The Collector stood there, torn as to what to do. He had learned over the years to trust his instincts, and they were telling him that he was in no immediate danger. He looked around at the desolate landscape, then followed the old man into the church.

TWO

The old man lit candles, illuminating the broken interior of the church. Old pews still lined one side of the room, the other side mostly rubble. There was a faded painting of Jesus on the wall and a large wooden crucifix, another dusty monument in a place where long-dead gods were worshipped. Nobody believed in such deities anymore. Nobody believed any supreme being could allow them to live on in such a brutal and hopeless world in cruel and hopeless conditions.

"Sit down, sit down. Take a load off," the old man said as he walked. He was hunched over and walked with a limp as he lit more candles.

The Collector walked to one of the pews which has been arranged near to a small coal-powered stove. The old man sat, folding his bony, dirt-pitted hands and looked at the Collector, his face a ghastly dance of shadows in the flickering candlelight.

"So you say you want to see the ocean?" the old man said, his voice echoing through the broken remains of the church.

The Collector remained silent. Although he had no reason not to trust the old man, there were too many dark, shadowy recesses in the old building for him to feel comfortable.

"Don't say much, do ye, son?" the old man said, pulling up an old stool. "Well, can't says I blame ye. Maybe that's the best way to be in this world."

"The ocean...you said you've seen it?" the Collector said, his voice echoing around the cavernous space.

The old man nodded. "I used to work on it, or at least back before the event."

"I don't remember it, before, I mean."

"No, you wouldn't. How old are ye, son?" the old man said.

"I don't know."

"Got a name?"

The Collector shook his head.

"No name, eh? Very strange." The old man rubbed his chin, his eyes glimmering in the gloom. "Well, my name's McCarthy."

He held out a gnarled hand. The Collector looked at it, confused and unsure what to do.

"Never done a handshake, eh?" McCarthy chuckled and lowered his hand back to his lap. "Yeah, the world ain't what it used to be that's for sure."

"What was it like before?"

McCarthy considered the question. He closed his eyes, pale tongue flicking side to side as he licked his lips. "Well, it was fuller, that's for sure. Lots of people, lots of noise. Everyone trying to scheme and steal, beg and borrow. It was a filthy, violent place until the event happened."

The Collector nodded. Everyone had different explanations of the event, but nobody knew for sure what it was or how it happened. All that was certain was the absolute devastation left behind. "What was it like?"

"The event?"

The Collector nodded. McCarthy didn't answer. He struggled to open a can of beans, his arthritic hands making hard work of the can opener. "Sorry, the ol' hands don't work so good anymore." He handed the can to the Collector, who took it but didn't eat.

"Well, go right ahead," McCarthy said, handing over a grubby spoon. "I've already eaten today."

Trust was now a secondary thing to hunger. He ate the beans, juice dribbling into his beard as the old man watched, a wry smile on his face. "You enjoy that now. No need to rush."

He changed position and drummed a spindly finger on his leg. "So, you want to know about the event, eh?"

The Collector nodded.

"Well, truth is, nobody knows what it was. I doubt anyone will ever find out now anyways. I suppose all those who might know about it are long dead by now. All I can tell you is my experience of it."

McCarthy stared off into the distance, recalling old memories. "We had no warning. Nobody knew anythin' about it till it happened. I used to have a farm, a few fields, and cattle. We made our livin' on the livestock. We had the best-bred cows in the area, and soon as they went to slaughter, demand was high. Anyways, this one day I was out in the back field, preparin' for the harvest. I hear a noise. At first, I think it's a plane or something. Then it turns into a high-pitched whine. Real loud, real intense. My wife, Vivian, God rest her soul, had come to the door, soap suds on her hands. She looked at me, I looked at her, and then we both looked to the sky."

He cleared his throat, bottom lip trembling as he recalled it.

"There was a white flash. Real bright. Lit up the sky and stayed that way for days, then that smell, that burnin' smell that is everywhere now drifted to us on the wind."

"What happened then?"

McCarthy looked at the ground. "Everyone died. My wife fell down at the door. My neighbour, Franklin, had been ploughing his field in the big red harvester he had. He slumped forward at the controls, the harvester rolling to a halt. Even that wasn't the worst."

"What happened?" the Collector said, food forgotten, a spoonful of beans held halfway to his mouth.

"The animals," McCarthy said. "My dog, Patch, made this god-awful noise and collapsed down, dead. Then the birds came. Like little black bullets as far as the eye could see, falling out of the sky, struck down in mid-flight by the event. I saw a plane go down, commercial jet. I guess the pilots were killed by whatever the hell the event was. It speared towards the ground, rotating over and over in slow circles. I didn't see the impact, but I did see the fireball."

"A man told me a few years ago that it was a bomb."

McCarthy shook his head. "I don't know what it was, but I know what it wasn't, and let me tell you, it wasn't no bomb. There was no noise, no explosion. Just that flash, that smell, then everything died. First the people, then the plants and the trees, the grasses. Whatever happened sterilised this place. Why we didn't die with the rest, I don't know though."

McCarthy sat reflective as the Collector continued to eat his beans. Neither of them spoke for a while. When the Collector had finished, he put the spoon inside the empty can and set it at his feet. "How do I get to the ocean?"

McCarthy frowned. "Well, I'm not so sure you should be goin' there at all, truth be known. Nothin' to do with me of course, just sayin' I wouldn't go there."

"Why?"

"Because it ain't like your picture no more, that's why," McCarthy snapped, then stood quickly, striding to the door and staring out into the dead world beyond. "I'm sorry about that," he said quietly, "but I don't like to think about it too much…but, it seems if you're insistin' on going there, I should warn you to be careful. If you want to go look, then that's fine, no problem with that. But if you plan to go out there…" The old man turned and looked at the Collector, old eyes tired and filled with partially forgotten fear. "Well, maybe I wouldn't do that. Wait here, I want to show you somethin'."

McCarthy hobbled into the darkness of the church. The Collector waited while he scratched around in an old chest of junk. He came back with a large bundle wrapped in rags. He sat down, setting the bundle across his knees. It was large and bulky. The Collector looked at it, then at McCarthy. The old man's face was tense and devoid of emotion.

"I saw a man ten years ago on the road about, maybe, a hundred miles from here," McCarthy said. "He was walking, his clothes all covered in dry blood. His arm was a mess. It had been cut, shredded, actually, and the infection had set in. Flies had already laid eggs in it, and his rotten skin was already full of maggots. Anyways, he begs me to help him, says he needs medical supplies. 'Course, anyone who looked at that arm would know it was beyond savin', but you couldn't say that. Wasn't my place to. I had a good place then, a little house tucked away from anyone who might be lookin'. I told the guy I'd do my best to fix him up. I cleaned the arm, put some bandages on it. Nothing that could actually help him, ye understand. But it made him feel better. Anyways, he readies to leave, and he says he wants to give me somethin' to say thanks for helpin' him. He opens his bag and takes this out."

McCarthy patted the large bundle of rags on his lap. The old man stared at the Collector, one bony hand still on the bundle. "Says he took it from somethin' he found washed up on the beach. I asked him what it was, but he just handed me this, said I should have it. He said he couldn't give me anything of value, cos' he didn't have anythin' on him. He said he could give me this information though, and said I should keep it in mind if ever I thought about going out on the ocean."

"What is it?" the Collector asked, unable to take his eyes off the bundle.

"No words can describe it. Best I just show ye."

McCarthy unwrapped the bundle, his movements slow and careful. The Collector leaned closer, looking at the object within.

"What is it?" he asked.

"That's a tooth, son."

The Collector glanced at McCarthy, then back at the object, unable to comprehend what he was looking at.

It was around eleven inches long, and curved to a dagger-tip point. It was white and looked brittle. Towards the thickest end, a huge blackish root, which was the size of both of the Collector's fists together. Mesmerised, he reached out to touch it.

"Careful, son," McCarthy said. "See the edges? Serrated."

The Collector withdrew his hand, and looked closer at the tooth, noting that, exactly as McCarthy has said, the edges of the tooth were still incredibly sharp.

"That thing would slice your skin to the bone. Very sharp. Very dangerous."

"I've never seen anything like it," the Collector mumbled, unable to take his eyes from the tooth.

"Nobody has, or at least, not that I know of. But that man swore to me the thing this had come from, the rotten carcass he found washed up on the sand, was huge. He said it was enough to stop him ever wanting to go in the water ever again. He said even though it was rotten and stinkin', the corpse on the beach was huge. I mean, hell, you only have to look at this tooth to know that."

"But what is it? I mean, what is it from?"

McCarthy hesitated, watching the Collector for what felt to him like very long time.

"Who knows," he shrugged, wrapping the tooth again. "All I know is what I told you. Maybe it's something that evolved after the event. Something new, something nobody has ever seen before."

"What happened to the man?"

McCarthy shrugged. "I fixed him up and he and I parted ways. I never saw him again. I like to think he made it, but based on that arm wound, I reckon he's almost definitely dead now."

The Collector nodded as McCarthy set the wrapped tooth on the floor beside him. "What about you, son?" he said. "What's your next move?"

"I don't know. I'll just keep going."

McCarthy nodded again, those sharp eyes probing. "You know, you could stay here. There's plenty of room, plus I have food. I could use a strong kid like you to help fix up the place."

"No, thanks, I need to keep moving."

"For what? There ain't nothin' out there, just look at it."

The Collector looked over his shoulder to the square of light showing the outside world. Brown, and barren, lead skies adding to the gloom.

"It's a damn wasteland out there, son, like in the movies."

"Movies? What are they?"

McCarthy half smiled in the gloom. "Well, back before the event, people called actors made films, uh, shows for people to watch. They pretended to be other people, some of them were good at it. Others, not so much. It was quite a big business."

The Collector frowned, and McCarthy's grin widened. "Well, I guess it all sounds stupid to someone like you who has only ever known this world like it is. Pity. I reckon you would have enjoyed it."

The Collector stood, eyes flicking to the wrapped tooth by McCarthy's chair. "I have to go."

"You don't have to rush off yet. Stay a while. It's a lonely world out there."

"I can't, I have to move on."

"Why? There ain't nothing there, I already told you."

The Collector had no answer. He didn't know why, all he knew was that he had to go. There was no choice. He felt compelled to keep moving, to find something that both made sense and justified his existence in the world. "Thanks for the food," he said, then walked towards the door.

"Now wait just a second." McCarthy said, standing and retreating back into the dark. The Collector waited, listening to the old man scratch around in the dark. He came back with five silver cans.

"Here," he said handing the cans over. "At least take these with you. Just beans, nothin' fancy, but its food."

"Thank you," the Collector said, shrugging out of his backpack and putting the cans inside. "Are you sure you have enough?"

"Wouldn't have given you them if I didn't, now would I?"

"Thanks," the Collector grumbled, unsure how to handle the old man's kindness.

"Which way you goin'?"

The Collector looked out of the door. Every direction looked much the same. Desolate. Cold. Dead. He shrugged. "Not sure."

"Don't give me that bull," McCarthy grunted. "You're still lookin' for the ocean, ain't ye?"

The Collector didn't answer. He just looked at McCarthy, not wanting to lie to someone who had been so generous. The old man flicked his head to the left. "That way. Keep walking and in maybe, five or six days, you'll find what you're looking for."

"Thanks," the Collector said, stepping out into the stinking, dull day. "For everything."

"Now you listen," McCarthy said, following the Collector outside. "You'll be safe to stay on the road for maybe a day or so, but as soon as you reach the outskirts of the next town, you get off it, you hear me? You stick to the side roads, make sure you keep low. Actually, wait a second."

He retreated back inside the broken church. The Collector waited, listening to the dull sounds of him rummaging around. He came back, red-faced and out of breath. "Here."

He handed the Collector a tattered, taped-together map. It had been drawn on by McCarthy over the years and was almost falling apart.

"That red dot is here, where we are no," the old man said, pointing at the red blob on the map. "You're facin' that way, down the road." He traced a line with his finger down the road on the map. "See here, where this red X is?"

The Collector nodded.

"That's where you need to get off the road. There's a marker there, three cars stacked on top of each other right across the right side of the road. There, you'll see a dirt road to the left leadin' into the trees. You wanna take that road. It takes a bit longer, but you at least avoid *them*."

"Who?"

"Bad people, son. Bad people. See this town?"

He pointed to a small cluster of buildings beyond the red X on the map. "Bad place, bad people. I've heard all kinds of stories about what they do to people, stuff I don't want to go into now.

All you need to know is that my way is safer. Look."

He moved his finger back to the X and traced a smaller line which cut off to the right. "See?" he said as he drew his finger through the woods marked on the fragile paper and out of the other side beyond the town. "You go my way, you avoid them and get to live a little longer. Once you're past the town, re-join the road and go maybe, another ten miles or so, and you should see the ocean. Whatever you do, keep your eyes open. You can never be too careful, especially where strangers are concerned."

The Collector looked at the map, then back to McCarthy. "Did you make this?"

The old man chuckled. "Not me, my hands don't work so good like I said. My brother made it. We found the map, we just made our own markings on it back when we were like you and thought there might be somethin' out there still to find."

"You have a brother?"

McCarthy's brow furrowed, and he looked at the floor. "Not anymore. Not since Gerry found that damn town, which is why I'm advising you to keep away from it. He didn't and paid the price for it. Got himself killed."

"I'm sorry."

"I am too. Be safe, son. Even though it's not as full as it once was, there are still some bad, bad people in this world."

"Thank you, for everything," the Collector said, hopping off the stoop, his feet kicking up a cloud of dust. He paused, staring down the endless pencil line of road which melted into the distance. He glanced at McCarthy, nodded and set off on his way.

INTERLUDE TWO
THE BEAST WITHIN

I saw it.

I saw it rise out of the ocean, a behemoth, a monstrous thing that had no place even in this broken world.

AMALGAMATION

It might have once been shark, or whale, or octopus at one time, but not anymore, now it's something new. Something merged together by the event. Like candle wax melting, so its flesh is bonded together creating something new. How it lives is a mystery. All I know is that I looked into its black eyes and saw death.

It came towards the boat, quivering and lurching, somehow propelling its unnatural form through the water. My men and I could only stand there and stare at the horrific and somehow beautiful scale of the beast as it passed beneath our boat. Silently, as if one man, we crossed from the port side to the starboard, so we could continue to watch as it went on its way. In all my years on the ocean, never have I seen such a thing. I knew then, as we raced for shore, that the ocean is no longer a place for man. I promised myself after that day I would never again venture onto the oceans and instead find my sustenance elsewhere.

IN THE FLESH

The flesh of man, those who scavenge and haunt these broken lands. It is in them that we will find our sustenance. Why should we, the strong, venture out onto the oceans and face such deadly beasts, when the weak are so plentiful and easy to harvest? Is this not our only option? Our crops are dead and animals spoiled and extinct. Only man remains.

NATURAL SELECTION

The strong survive and the weak falter. This has been the way through all history.

ONLY THE STRONG

We shall take them and harvest them like cattle. We shall pack them into cages and fatten them. This will not be done with cruelty, but to ensure survival for we, the strong.

REJOICE IN THE FLESH!

Meat, glorious meat. A thigh, a rump, a rack of ribs roasted over an open fire. Enough to make one salivate, enough to make a man forget the horrors he has seen in the ocean.

I met another man who encountered the same thing as I. He spoke of his boat being capsized, his crew taken by one of those awful creatures from the deepest pit of hell. He spoke of the ocean bubbling as if on fire, a pool of boiling chaos from which the hellish beast was spewed. Thirty feet of it he said, and I believe him. The dimensions of the one I saw was comparable in scale. I wish the man and I could have conversed for longer, but there are bellies to be filled and he was weak.

VITALITY

The surge in energy, the renewed vigour from the taste of fresh meat is irreplaceable. One of our number is a butcher, and he showed us how to make the most of the meat, how to ensure nothing was wasted or left that could be used. I asked our chef how he had sweetened the meat so, and he replied that it was nothing he had done. I wonder if perhaps fear led to that delightful sweetness. With belly full and body rested, our thoughts turn to our next feed. People are becoming thinner and thinner spread, and as such, our new food source may become harder to find.

TRUST

That is the key. People as a rule are trusting. We should use this to our advantage. It would, I think be quite simple. An offer of shelter, a promise of warmth and food, all things that the people of the new world need in order to function. They will come to us, and we will never need to hunt again.

REJOICE IN THE FLESH!

For it is the life. For the strong, it is a means to continue, and to keep us from having to venture out onto the seas where those twisted, bastardised things dwell. This is the way, this is the light, and this is how we are to survive. This world is no longer ours to rule, we no longer sit on top of the food chain.

BASTARDISATION

There are new masters of this planet, twisted, mutated things that prowl the black seas in search of blood and flesh. No longer must we abide by the rules of society, no longer must we pretend to be civil to our fellow man. The flesh is food, and food is survival. We will build a new world from the bones of the dead and call it home.

This is the way of the new world. This is the way of the future.

CHAPTER THREE

The rain had been falling all night and most of the day, and as a result, the Collector felt dirty. It was a stagnant, greasy substance, and left a slimy sheen on the skin; its taste was also bitter and oily, tinged with the ash-like sulphur taste as always. With nowhere to shelter, the Collector walked on, trudging through the mud down the road which he hoped would eventually lead him to the ocean. McCarthy's kindness had not been easy to forget. In a world of cruelty, such selflessness was impossible to ignore. He stopped, hands on hips and stared at the horizon. In the distance, he could see the town he had been warned about, the white, low buildings, formless and without any semblance of life from such a distance. A little further down the road, the stacked cars were exactly where McCarthy had said they would be, by the side of the road, beyond which the dead forest waited. He stared at the trees, the new growths of leaves twisted and changed into bulbous shapes which were inedible. This he had noticed more of late. Some trees from the old world remained dead and barren, others took on new life. He wondered if they were that way because they were drinking the same water he was collecting to consume later. It wasn't something worth thinking about, nor were the consequences if proved true, and so he focused on the task at hand and what he intended to do next. He approached the stacked cars, the rusted shells as dead and broken as the rest of the world. He stopped beside them, their mass giving him a brief respite from the horrific weather conditions. The trail was barely visible snaking into the trees. It would be easy to miss had he not known to look for it. He glanced again towards the town and remembered McCarthy's words about the kind of people who lived there. People he most definitely wanted to avoid. Decision made, he peeled off into the dead tangle of trees.

TWO

The forest was absolutely silent now that the rain had stopped. No birds had sung within those trees for years, just as no animals existed to make their home there anymore. Now it was a cold, haunting place, the only sound the brittle snap of long-dead branches on the ground as the Collector stepped on them. The trail wound itself parallel to the road, snaking downhill and keeping him hidden from view of the town, which was somewhere to his right. After the rain had stopped, a light mist had formed and was hanging around his feet as he made his way deeper through the trees, his every sense alive and attuned to his surroundings. Something caught his eye, something pinned to a tree, its corner flapping when it caught the breeze. The words on it were printed in block capitals as if the person who wrote it wanted to ensure his point was listened to. The Collector walked towards the poster pinned to the tree and stared at the words, letting them sink in.

FROM THE FIRES OF HELL THEY CAME! TWISTED THINGS, AMALGAMATIONS OF THE LORDS BEAUTIFUL CREATIONS TWISTED INTO TERRIBLE, TERRIBLE THINGS.

DEMONS!

DEMONS FROM THE DEEP. I SAW IT WITH MY OWN EYES, AND I KNEW THAT NO PRAYERS WOULD BE

LOUD ENOUGH, NO FAITH WOULD BE STRONG ENOUGH. I SAW THE DEVIL. I SAW IT PULL THOSE POOR PEOPLE OFF THE DOCK.

ABOMINATION!

NEVER HAVE I SEEN SUCH A FREAK OF NATURE. NEVER HAVE I WITNESSED SOMETHING TO TWISTED AND SO DISFIGURED. I SAW ITS EYES, AND PRAISE JESUS I SAW ITS MAW, RINGED WITH FANGS, WHICH WAS ENOUGH TO MAKE MY BLOOD RUN COLD. THAT CREATURE SPITS IN THE FACE OF ALL THAT HIS HOLY.

THE END HAS COME!

THE END HAS COME AND WE WILL ALL ANSWER TO OUR MAKER!

WE WILL ALL BURN, WE WILL ALL SUFFER. WE WILL ALL FACE JUDGEMENT. THE DEMONS FROM THE DEEP WILL SEE TO THAT!

PRAY TO THEM, PRAY TO THEM AND BEG FOR MERCY. BEG FOR FORGIVENESS. BEG FOR OUR LORD TO GRANT US PASSAGE TO HEAVEN. BEG FOR HIS MERCY FROM THE ABOMINATIONS OF THE DEEP. PRAY FOR HIS LOVE TO GUIDE US INTO THE LIGHT AND THE WARMTH OF THE SUN.

PRAY!

FOR IF YOU DO NOT THEN THOSE THINGS WILL

TAKE YOU AND DRAG YOU DOWN TO THE HELL FROM WHERE THEY CAME. PRAY WITH ME, PEOPLE. PRAY FOR THE SUN TO BRING LIFE BACK TO THE EARTH. PRAY FOR FORGIVENESS AND THE WARMTH OF HIS LIGHT. SPREAD THE WORD TO ALL WHO MIGHT LISTEN.

PRAY!

He read it twice, then a third time. The words tied into the story McCarthy had told him about the man he had met on the road, and the giant tooth he had been shown. For the first time, the Collector was having second thoughts about going to the ocean. For so long it had been his goal, his dream, something that kept him going, that kept him trying to survive. If such things could exist, and if they were more than just stories, then it might be better for him to forget the idea completely. A second thought came to him that he could at least go and see it, that even if such things did exist, they couldn't harm him from the land. He could at least go and see the ocean, to see if it was like the postcard he had found. That, at least he could do. A distant snap of laughter rolled to him through the trees, breaking his train of thought. He dropped to one knee, staring through the tangle of long-dead wood, trying to pinpoint where it was coming from. More voices now, snatches of words echoing towards him from the direction of the road. He put his bag on the ground and crouched, keeping low and cautious as he inched closer to take a look.

There were two men on the road walking from the direction of the town. They looked like everyone else. Dirty, wretched, desperate. One of them had a machete, the blade dirty and covered with blood. The Collector pushed himself against the ground, wishing he hadn't moved so close to the road. The men walked passed his position, none of them glancing in his direction. He waited until they were gone, then scrambled back towards the trail. He put his backpack on and continued on his way, desperate now to get the town behind him. He glanced back over his shoulder, aware that anyone could be sneaking up on him and he would have no idea until it was too late. He had grown used to being alone in the world and knew he had to start considering the other people who existed within it and what they might do. It was as he had that thought that he stepped in the trap. Triggered by his weight, the snare tightened around his ankle and pulled him into the air, leaving him hanging upside down by one leg, his bag spilling its contents onto the ground underneath him. Panic set in as the snare dug into his ankle. He took a breath, watching his upside-down world twist and spin. It was then that they appeared, the men from the road. One was bald, a huge, filthy, ginger beard hanging down to his chest. One eye was pointed inwards towards his nose, the other glaring hard. His machete-wielding friend was just watching, enjoying watching the Collector spin and twist.

"Looks like we caught us a little somethin', Eric," he said, walking closer.

The Collector said nothing, watching and unable to take his eyes from the machete. Its owner saw him looking and smiled. "Don't worry about this little thing; it won't hurt you unless you piss me off."

The Collector flailed and tried to squirm free as the man swung the machete at the wire holding him in the air. He crumbled to the ground, landing on the head, the impact knocking him unconscious.

INTERLUDE THREE:
NOT ENOUGH TIME IN THE WORLD

He wasn't going to make it.

Jansen knew it, but was determined to try all the same. He swerved in and out of traffic, the silver Mercedes oblivious to the irritated honking of other drivers. He carved in and around them, questionable manoeuvre after questionable manoeuvre as he desperately tried to reach home in time.

It was rush hour, and the city was alive with lights and activity. People were finishing work and looking forward to the weekends, the bars and restaurants already filling up. It was impossible to warn them, impossible to help them or tell them those things would never happen. A glance at the clock on the radio display said it was a little after five in the evening. He calculated how long he had, the answer terrifying him.

It wasn't enough. Not even close.

Determined not to give up, he pushed the accelerator harder to the floor.

His normal thirty-minute journey was completed in twelve minutes. His home was in the Los Angeles hills, a sprawling glass-and-steel structure with a pool and hot tub. It was expensive, but he could afford it. The job had paid him well and was one he had never considered the implications of until everything went wrong just over an hour ago. He skidded to a halt, leaving the engine running and racing for the house, Italian shoes crunching on gravel as he threw open the door.

"Sarah? Mikey?"

"In here."

He followed the sound of his wife's voice to the main sitting room. It was a large open space, crème furniture and red rugs, two of the three walls floor-to-ceiling glass, giving a stunning view of the Los Angeles skyline, which glittered far below them.

He glanced at it, knowing what was coming and feeling the pressure of time with each passing second.

His wife, Sarah, sat with their two children. Ten-year-old Mikey, who was playing Xbox, and their nine-month-old daughter, Skye.

Sarah immediately saw it on his face. The despair. The fear.

"What is it, what happened? Why are you home so early?" she asked.

We have to go, right now," he snapped.

Both of them were looking at him, and he knew how he must look and sound.

"I don't understand…"

"Move, now, go get in the car."

"What's happening? Where are we going?"

He didn't answer, not because he didn't want to, but because he had couldn't. There was nowhere to go, nowhere to run where they would be safe. He had never told her the specifics of his job, in part because it was classified, but also because he knew she would look at him differently if she knew what he actually did. He had no time to explain, no time to sit her down and go into detail about what had happened and about how every wasted second brought them all closer to death. He took a breath and tried to keep calm.

"Just move. Now, Mikey, come on.

"Shall I pack a bag?" Sarah asked, eyes wide and filled with questions as she stood and moved the baby to the opposite arm.

Jansen shook his head. "No, we don't have time. In the car now, move it, we have to –"

A shrill alarm carried up the hillside from the heart of the city and stopped him mid-sentence.

"Jansen, What is it? What's going on?" Sarah asked.

He didn't answer her. All the fight, all the urgency had gone out of him. He walked over to the large windows, and looked down over his three-million-dollar view. All those people. All those lives about to end.

"It's too late," he muttered.

"What is? What are you talking about?"

He tried to look for the lab, his place of work that had afforded him the lifestyle, the house and would ultimately end it. He couldn't see specific details amid the glow of the streetlights, but knew roughly where it was in the sprawling mass of buildings below. He waited for it.

"It's too late," he muttered, his face now inches from the glass.

"What is? What are you talking about late? Too late for who?"

"Everyone," he whispered.

That was when it happened. A pinprick of light, soundless and growing from the lab, a soundless explosion of energy which he knew would go on indefinitely. The light grew brighter, and a high-pitched whine filled the air. Skye began to cry. For her at least, there would be blissful ignorance about what was to come.

Jansen sensed Sarah beside him. He reached out and took her hand in his and waited as the light came closer.

He closed his eyes and silently wept as it grew more intense. "Don't be afraid," he whispered. "It won't hurt."

Then, there was darkness.

Then, there was silence.

CHAPTER FOUR

It was the smell he noticed first. A sour, ammonia stench. The Collector coughed and opened his eyes, blinking through the gloom. He was in a cage, wire mesh and filthy. He rolled over onto his side, staring at the hazy figure who sat on a wooden chair, staring at him. It took a few seconds for his brain to unscramble itself and figure out what he was looking at. He looked at the man, and the man looked back, leaning closer so that the shadows moved from his features and allowed a closer view of his face.

The Collector sat up, blinking and unable to believe what he was seeing.

McCarthy grinned. "They always have that look," he said.

The pleasant tone from his voice was gone. Unlike earlier, there was no hospitality, no kindness. This, the Collector realised, was the real McCarthy. Behind him stood the two men who had passed on the road. Now that they were all standing together, the resemblance was impossible to ignore. The two men shared similar features to their father, the same eyes and hooked nose.

McCarthy sat patiently, letting the Collector figure it all out. "Don't worry about it, son," he said, unleashing his wicked grin. "You're not the first and you won't be the last. Don't beat yourself up about it."

The Collector shook his head. "I don't understand."

"Hit your head pretty good, didn't ye?" the old man chuckled, then leaned closer, propping his elbows on his knees. "My boys did good, just like they always do. Before we go any further, I reckon I ought to at least be straight with you."

He reached behind him and held out a scrawny hand. The bigger of McCarthy's sons, the one called Eric, handed his father the map. McCarthy unfolded it, and showed it to the Collector.

"Remember this?"

The Collector looked at it and said nothing. Of course he remembered.

"You're the seventeenth person to be brought to us by this map. You people are too gullible, that's the problem. Seems to me like whatever it was that killed the world left a lot of stupid people behind. Just know this is nothin' personal, son. It's just circumstances. Just know that you'll die to make sure my family and me can go on. Look at it this way, you have a purpose in life at least that isn't some stupid idea of finding the sea." McCarthy chuckled as he said it and sat up straight.

"Please, I didn't do anything to you," the Collector said.

"No, you didn't," McCarthy said. He looked almost apologetic behind the cruel exterior. "And for that, I'm sorry. But this world ain't what it once was. We gotta survive anyway we can."

He pointed a finger, the slight shift in position throwing shadows back across this face. "The weak have to go first. It's as simple as that. If you'd have been strong, if you'd have been wise, you would have killed me up at the church. Now, like the rest, you'll have to pay the price."

"Please…"

"No, don't try and talk your way out of it. I gave you every chance to off me up there. Showed you my back, gave you an advantage, but you didn't take it. You trusted me. Ain't no place for behaving like that in this world. None at all. The weak defer to the strong. That's the way it's always been, that's how it will go on. Now you and the rest will finally serve a purpose. You'll finally have your place."

"The others?" the Collector repeated, confused.

56

McCarthy grinned again, the sat upright. "Boys, open the shutters for our guest. Let him see the rest of his new home."

Eric and his sibling each moved off into the shadows, peeling away from McCarthy, who kept his eyes on the Collector. A grind of metal as unoiled chains were pulled and shutters lifted, spilling light into the room.

The Collector blinked and looked around the room. It was a warehouse filled with mouldy boxes which would never be distributed. There were four other cages like his. Two of them were empty, the others contained people, one man, and one woman. The Collector looked at them and saw his future. They were afraid and filthy, cowering in the corner of their respective cages and sitting in their own filth. They didn't make eye contact with their captors, and the Collector could see that they had been beaten into submission, both mentally and physically. The man, who looked to be somewhere in his forties, was overweight. Empty bean cans like the one McCarthy had given to the Collector littered the floor of his cage. McCarthy saw him looking and chuckled.

"See him? He's fattening up nicely. Was skinny as a rake when he got here, a lot like you are now. We'll soon fix that though."

"I don't understand," the Collector said again, glancing from his fellow captives to McCarthy.

"That might be for the best, son. Startin' today, you're on five meals a day. Only beans I'm sorry to say. It's pretty much all this place had when we found it. Tins of the damn things in the thousands. You behave yourself and do as you're told, we'll all get along fine. You step out of line, then I'll have to get Eric and Glynn here to beat some humility into you."

Glynn, the one only known to the Collector as the man wielding the machete, approached and shoved an open can of beans between the bars. "Make sure you eat all of that. Every bit."

The Collector took the can, holding on to it and still trying to figure out what to do.

"Alright," McCarthy said, standing and stretching. "I have to get back to the church. Don't let me hear about you steppin' out of line. You're a nice kid; I'd hate to have something happen to you."

"Please," the Collector said, "We talked. About the man you helped, about your brother."

"That we did," McCarthy said, grimacing and rubbing his knee. "But they were just words."

"Please…"

"Enough. You eat up now. I'd hate to hear the boys had to hurt you." McCarthy walked towards the exit of the storeroom, his sons following and closing the steel sliding door, plunging the room into silence. The Collector looked at the man and the woman, neither of them looking at him. It seemed that whatever demons they were dealing with, they were unwilling to include him. He looked at the can of beans. His stomach growled in need, and even though he knew what eating would entail in the long term, he couldn't resist. He scooped his fingers into the open can and started to eat.

TWO

Two days and nights came and went, and no words had been spoken. In regular intervals, McCarthy's sons would bring each of them a new tin of beans and remove the old can. It was machine-like. It was on the third day that the silence was broken.

"You know why we're here, don't you?"

The Collector turned to the woman. She was still cowering in the corner of her cage, her filthy skin crusted with dried blood. Her eyes were frightened, her hair greasy. It was hard to tell if she was attractive or not. Under the circumstances, it really didn't matter. He shook his head.

"You stopped at the church didn't you, on the edge of the town?"

The Collector nodded.

"I did too," the woman said, gripping on to the bars with a delicate, filthy hand. "The old man was really nice. Really sweet. He gave me food, let me stay the night in the church. He talked to me, listened to me. Asked me where I was heading and where I wanted to go. I said I was looking for somewhere safe. The next day, he gave me a map, told me to avoid the town, but that I'd be safe if I went a different way."

"Through the woods?" the Collector said.

"Through the woods," she repeated. "It's how they do it. The old man sends people that way on purpose. He gains their trust, tells them that whatever it is you are looking for is on the other side of that town. Then the traps get you, and they bring you here. That's what they did to us."

The Collector looked passed her to the man in the other cage.

"No, not him. I don't know who he is," the woman said. She nodded towards the empty cage. "They took my friend the other day they…" Her lip started to tremble, and she rested her head on the bars.

"What happened?" the Collector asked.

"They ate her." There was nothing resembling emotion in her voice. No humanity. He looked at her, trying to process, and slowly realising how the operation worked.

"You get it now, don't you?" the woman said. "We're livestock. Animals just waiting to be eaten. They fatten us up, feed us beans all day until we're ready for slaughter. It's not worthwhile to them if we're skinny."

The Collector looked at her, then at the man who was ignoring them both, his eyes focused on the golden light of freedom out of the windows.

"He was your size when he was brought in," the woman said, following his line of sight. "Skinny and underfed. Look at him now, fat and ready to eat. Enough to go around and last a while they'll come for him soon. Then it will be our turn to wait."

She looked the Collector up and down. "You might be lucky, for a while at least. Might take time to fatten you up. Same with me. With any luck, they'll find someone else before then, someone fat, someone ready to butcher straight away. This is pretty much a store room."

"McCarthy said he used to have a farm, breed cattle for slaughter," the Collector said.

"And that never stopped. Just instead of cattle, he's moved on to humans."

The Collector looked around the store room. "What about escape?"

She laughed. A single shrill bark. The man in the other cage glanced at her then returned to staring out of the window.

"You don't get it. There is no escape. We can't get out of here. All we can do is wait to die. There are a lot of them out there to feed. Fighting is hopeless against a whole town."

She turned away from him, facing the corner. The Collector settled down, hoping she was wrong, even though all the evidence pointed to everything she said being correct.

THREE

They came for the man on the fifth day. McCarthy's two sons,

Glynn and Eric took him. He kicked and screamed, trying desperately to cling onto his filth-caked cage, but they were too strong for him, and he was dragged out of the holding room, the steel door slamming closed and cutting off his pained screams. The Collector stared wide eyed. The woman paid it no attention. She had seen this before.

The idea that had been forming in his head over the last few days had become something he would have to risk. He couldn't wait any more. He glanced at the woman, guilt stabbing at him. He would help her if he could, but the truth was he probably wouldn't be able to, unless his suspicions were correct. He switched position, avoiding the corner of his cage which he had been forced to use as a toilet. The stinking mess a reminder of just how degrading the conditions were in which they were expected to live. He looked at the empty cans which littered the ground. Every few hours, they would bring them, forcing them to eat. He was already feeling lethargic as he took on more food than he had ever eaten in his life. He saw the strategy now. Fatten them up and make sure they are too slow and overweight to fight back. It was actually clever. Why should they hunt for food when human nature made it easy for them to just lead their potential meals to them? The woman had told him they would be in to hose them down later, which was as close to a chance to clean up as they were likely to get. He looked at the stinking pile of excrement in the corner and hoped it would be soon.

The shadows were long when Eric came. He sauntered into the room, dragging a tatty red hose behind him.

"Lucky we've had so much rain, or you would be sittin' in your shit for a bit longer," he said as he dropped the hose on the floor and approached the cages. The smell didn't seem to be bothering him. The Collector supposed he was used to it by now. He looked at the woman first, greedy eyes crawling all over her body. "You ain't fattening up so good, bitch," he grunted. "We might have to up your intake."

"I can't eat anymore, it's making me sick."

"Why ain't you getting fat?" Eric said, glaring at her through the bars as if it was something she was doing deliberately.

She was wise not to answer; instead, she lowered her head and retreated into the corner. Eric glanced at the Collector, but said nothing. It was, after all, too early to complain about his own lack of weight gain.

"I guess we'll just have to wait a while," he said, returning to the hose and picking it up off the floor. "We still have enough of the fat guy left anyway to last us a while. Just don't think you'll get out of this by stayin' thin. Meat's meat after all. Now stand up."

She did it immediately. The Collector had no idea how long she had been captive, but she was obviously accustomed to the routine. She stood and crossed her arms over her body, leaning against the bars in the corner. The Collector stared, curious.

"Well, come on, I ain't got all day," Eric snapped, glaring at him.

The Collector followed suit, doing as the woman had done, standing in the corner, arms crossed across his chest.

"Alright, good. You do as you're told. You keep doing that, and everything will be just fine like my daddy told you." He positioned his feet, readying the hose, a half smile on his lips. "Alright, pigs, bath time."

Eric turned on the hose, the icy water blasting out at an incredible velocity. It slammed the woman against the bars. She grabbed on, coughing and choking, feet scrabbling on the floor as her waste was blasted passed her to the back of the room. Eric was grinning now, clearly enjoying his work. The Collector waited, bracing himself as Eric turned the hose on him. The cold hit him hard, driving the wind out of him. He grabbed the bars, coughing and spluttering, the sound of Eric's laughter still audible over the roar of the water. The Collector took a great breath then fell down, crumbling to the floor. He started to convulse, arms and legs kicking as he flopped around on the floor of his cage. Eric turned off the hose, dropping it to the floor.

"Hey, what's going on? You okay in there?" he said, staring into the cage.

The Collector lay on his front, unmoving, limbs splayed out.

"Hey, come on, get up. It's probably just the cold put you into shock, that's all," Eric said, sounding unconvinced. He didn't care about the Collector, of course. He did, however, care what his father would think if some of their livestock had died before they were ready to eat it.

"Fuck, fuck, fuck." He turned to the woman, who was trembling and sodden in her cage. "You saw I didn't do nothin', didn't you? You saw he just fell down. If my daddy asks…"

The woman said nothing. She didn't have to. The defiance in her eyes told him that he would get no sympathy or help from here. None at all.

"Jesus fuck. You fucking animals causing me trouble," Eric grunted. He walked over to the cage, fumbling for the keys in his pocket. He dropped them, picked them up and opened the cage.

"You okay, buddy? Don't you die, not yet. You need to stay awake for a while yet."

Erick grabbed the Collector under the arms and lifted his limp body up. It was then that he reacted. He lurched up, taking Eric by surprise, smashing the top of his head into the underside of Eric's jaw. The impact was devastating. Eric's head snapped back, slamming into the bars; somehow, he didn't go down.

"Glynn, get in here!" he screamed, his words woozy.

The Collector was also dizzy. Hot blood was running down his face from the wound in the top of his head where it had connected with Eric's jaw. It was getting into his eyes, stopping him from seeing.

"Glynn!" Eric screamed again.

There was no time to think, no time to do anything but act. The Collector took a half step towards Eric and grabbed his throat, squeezing with all the strength he could muster. He felt desperate fingers grabbing at his forearms, digging in for purchase. The blood mask now covered all of the Collector's face. He could hear it dripping onto the floor of the cage as Eric squirmed and kicked, choking and trying to take a precious breath.

The Collector couldn't see. There was too much blood in his eyes, in his mouth. He could hear well enough though. The desperate gasps, the ever-weakening clawing as Eric started to fade, his legs giving out as he lost his battle to breathe. The Collector released his grip, letting Eric slide down the bars into a slouched half-sitting position, bulging eyes staring into whatever awaited him in death.

The Collector wiped the blood from his eyes, the ever-increasing torrent of claret seemingly endless. He touched his hairline, feeling the jagged wound in the top of his skull. He knew he had done serious damage. Everything seemed slow and distant, his movements laboured. He had to move, had to act. He stumbled out of the cage, accompanied by the patter of blood on the concrete. He could hear footsteps from outside the room, running towards him. He knew he was in no condition for another physical battle. He was groggy and weak, and no fighter. He didn't like violence. He tried to get through life without conflict, but this, he reasoned, was different. This was about survival, and so what he did next was an instinctive decision. He scooped up the hose from the floor just seconds before Glynn entered the room. He saw the open cage, his brother slumped inside, but by then it was too late. The Collector stepped out behind him, looping the hose around his neck and pulling back with all the strength he had left. They stumbled around in lazy circles. The Collector blind due to the blood in his eyes, Glynn choking and clawing at the hose as he faced the same fate as his brother. Glynn had more fight, but ultimately stood no chance as his brain became starved of oxygen. He fell, pitching forward, his skull impacting the ground with sickening force, The Collector on top of him and continuing to pull the hose until he was sure Glynn was dead.

When it was done, he rolled off, exhausted, gasping and dizzy, again wiping blood from his eyes. He watched as it dripped onto the dirty concrete, pooling in front of him. He stumbled up, grabbing the keys which were still in the open door to his cage. He felt sick, and his vision was blurring as consciousness threatened to leave him. He couldn't allow that to happen. If he passed out, he was dead. Fighting to stay awake, he stumbled to the cage containing the woman, leaning on it for support. It took him three attempts to get the key into the hole. He opened the door, reaching out a hand.

"Come on, we have to go." His voice felt slow, distant. Like he was listening to someone else speak from far away.

The woman didn't move. She cowered and shook her head.

"Come on, we don't have time to waste," he said, another wave of nausea threatening to pull the ground from under him.

"The others will get you. They'll make you suffer," she gasped, staring past him at the bodies. She was scared. Scared of them, scared of *him*. He couldn't blame her. He could imagine how much of a mess he must look.

"Please, we have to go."

"There are too many of them. McCarthy said they have a

whole town. You can't win."

"Please, we have to try," he said, struggling to form his words.

She shook her head and clung to the bars of her cage, too afraid to risk going for freedom.

There was nothing else he could do. If he didn't move, he would pass out, and if that happened, he would die. He stumbled away from her, the room starting to sway, his vision dimming. He pushed through into the other room, distantly aware that if his suspicions were wrong, he was likely a dead man, the room beyond was a larger space. One area had been converted into a living area. Two dirty sofas sat around a table covered with faded pornographic magazines. The boxes of beans had been shaped into a functional living space of sorts. There were no other people, no town to feed. As he suspected, it was just McCarthy and his sons. They had talked about there being more as a means to keep their prisoners docile. It should have been obvious. Nobody but McCarthy's sons ever entered the room. Nobody else had ever been seen, and if there were more people to feed, they would have needed more cages, more people to fill them. They had gambled on people believing their story, and this time, their bluff had been called. Some clothes, dirty and grubby which obviously belonged to one of the brothers, were piled on top of one of the boxes. He took the first item, a faded green T-shirt, and pressed it to his head, a jolt of agony driving through him like lightning. He held it there, wiping the blood away with the other hand and finally able to see, and immediately wished he was still blind.

Beyond the living area was what he could describe only as a butchery. A steel table sat on top of plastic sheets. Beside it, a generator hummed, powering the lights, hose pump and the fridges. The carcass of the man was on the table. There was nothing left beneath the rib cage. His dead eyes stared from pale grey flesh. The man's innards were in a steel bucket by the table, one upper thigh bone stripped of meat propped beside it. The man's other leg was on the table, cleaver still embedded in it. This must have been where Glynn was working before his brother called for help.

The Collector felt his stomach vault once, twice. On the third, he vomited, a paste of bile and digested beans. His nausea was getting worse, his sense of control growing weaker. He had to go, had to escape before McCarthy came back. He stumbled past the sitting area, then the horrific kitchen. Behind that, two dirty bunks where the brothers slept stood empty and would forevermore. His backpack was on the floor by one of them. He stumbled over and picked it up, slinging it over his shoulder. At the end of the warehouse was the exit. The Collector stumbled towards it, leaning on boxes to help him, pausing every time he felt the nausea would be too much and wondering if he was out of time. His head screamed with pain, and even with the T-shirt to stem the flow, blood still seeped into his eyes. He wondered if the door would be locked, and half wished he had remembered to bring the ring of keys from the cage. He stumbled into the door, intending to rest before opening it, but to his surprise it fell open, and he landed hard on the floor outside on his hands and knees. He never thought he would be so grateful to smell that burnt-match smell, but in comparison to the horrors in the warehouse, it was the sweetest thing he had ever smelled. He took a second to get his bearings. In the distance, up the hill, he could see the white, half-collapsed church. Fear and anger conflicted within him, but he was in no condition to think about revenge. Instead, survival was key. Behind the warehouse, barren areas of dirt, which would once have housed crops and grasses, awaited him. Anything, he figured, was better than the woods. He set off in a half-stumbling walk, desperately trying to stay conscious. The day was drawing to a close, the light starting to fade from the day. He had no shelter, nowhere to rest. All he could do was keep going. He wasn't sure how long he walked for, or where he was. The town was far behind him, the night swallowing him and beckoning him closer with each stumbled step. The nausea was getting worse, and his head throbbed with an aggressive pain which made even keeping his eyes open a near impossibility. It was cold, his breath pluming as he walked. Ahead, more buildings loomed, shadowy husks of a long-dead town. He had learned now that these were places to be avoided, that the world still contained bad people even if the event had taken most of those who inhabited it. His feet hurt, the hard, dead earth making travel difficult. He stumbled, his ankle bending under him. He fell to his hands and knees, absolutely drained. Death didn't feel like such a bad prospect to him anymore. He thought it was something he could almost welcome. He closed his eyes and lay still, giving in to the need to rest, to the blackness that was so desperately trying to swallow him into oblivion. Within seconds, he was taken by the bliss of unconsciousness.

INTERLUDE FOUR:
EVERYTHING COMES WITH A PRICE

The wheelchair had started to squeak. For the last half mile of desolate, empty road, that repetitive sound had been second only to the sound of Sally's voice, neither of which seemed likely to stop anytime soon. She sat in the chair, hands clasped and twitching, chin slick with drool.

"I'm hungry," she whined, her voice nasal and slow, and difficult for most to understand.

Her dutiful sister, Delia, understood it well enough though. Since the day of the event five years earlier, she had been the only outlet for it. The older sibling by two years, the twenty-four-year-old knew not to react with anger. Instead, she half-tuned her sister down to a low whine and focussed instead on the sound of the wheel squeaking as they walked the endless road.

"You said you were taking me out, you said it would be somewhere nice," Sally said.

"We're out, aren't we?" Delia replied, trying to keep her cool and hide her anger, neither of which were easy when she was so mentally and physically exhausted. She pushed the wheelchair along, letting the tension between them simmer.

"You said it would be a special day. You don't care about me, just because I'm disabled you think I don't matter. I have rights, I should get special treatment."

Delia stopped pushing the chair. Her sister always did this and reverted to the disabled card when it suited her. She was bitter and selfish, and used the fact that she wasn't able-bodied to her advantage. Delia had tried to explain that the world was a different place now, but she was either unwilling or unable to comprehend it. It was times like this when Delia's frustrations came out in full force. "If you think you can do better on your own, be my guest," she snapped, hating herself for doing it immediately.

Silence.

Now even the chair wheel wasn't punctuating the quiet. Sally sat there for a moment, drooling and twitching, greasy hair flopping as she swung her head in involuntary movements. Delia knew well enough not to wait for an apology. They never came. Apparently being disabled meant she no longer had to have manners either. Instead, Delia resumed pushing the wheelchair down the edge of the road, the maddening squeak re-joining them.

"Just you remember who looks after you. Who washes you and cleans you, puts you on the toilet and finds us food and shelter. I'm doing the best I can. Your attitude doesn't help."

"But you promised we could go out. It's not fair. You never do anything nice for me."

Delia swallowed the things she wanted to say, the hateful, nasty things that were so desperate to come out. Instead, she looked out over the desolate land and took a deep breath. "I do the best I can for us, Sally. Just look around, the world is a mess. It's not all about you."

"It should be. I didn't ask to be like this. I should be a priority."

She once again fought the urge to react, and again let her eyes drift over the barren landscape. Everything was dark, washed out. There was a word for it that wouldn't come to her immediately, then arrived as she set her gaze on a snake of stationary rusting cars which had been at some point abandoned on the road.

Sterile.

That was the word she had been searching for. It had been only five years since everything changed, and she already struggled to remember anything of the old world. To think of it like it once was, so full and hectic, everybody moving with such urgency that they didn't care who they stepped on to do it, seemed alien to her. Stupid. It was easy to say now, of course, because things had changed beyond any comprehension. She was sure a mistake had been made, and those who survived the event had done so by accident. Surely its intention was to kill everyone, not leave a few wretched souls behind. The pair went on, Delia pushing her sister's wheelchair ahead of her, ignoring the skeletal remains which littered the streets. She had never seen a dead body before the incident, and now saw them as only part of the furniture of the new world. A sprinkling of garnish on earth's barren corpse. They didn't bother her. To her, they were the lucky ones.

"It's not fair. I'm disabled, my needs should come first," Sally said, apparently not content to let the point drop.

Delia knew she couldn't react, but was furious nonetheless. She had sacrificed everything to help her sister. It was always with her in mind that she did things that would have been unspeakable. Scavenging from the dead, or stealing from the weak just to make her sibling as comfortable as possible in a world where just survival alone was a luxury. She had endured countless nights with little or no sleep, and was always thinking forward to the next day and how they might get through it.

"Can you hear me? Don't ignore me."

"I hear you," Delia said. "We're going somewhere, aren't we?"

"But where? I'm cold. I'm hungry. This isn't fair. People like me should come first."

"Please, just give it a rest, will you? Just shut up and be quiet for five minutes, can you at least give me that?" She had snapped and knew it wouldn't help. She was well aware that her sister had become spoiled and craved constant attention. She had been that way before the event and seemed to have no intention of changing things now just because the world was dying.

"See? You resent me. You wish I were dead. Just because I'm disabled, you think I'm no use. It's not right, it's not fair. You hate me. Everyone should go out of their way to help people in my position."

"Look down there," Delia said, cutting her sister off. She pointed down the gentle slope of the road. At the bottom, a cluster of stalls made up a makeshift market. People who, from their vantage point, were tiny, scurried around and tried to bargain and barter for the things they needed to survive. "See? That's where we're going."

"The market? We came here last week. Besides, we don't have any money. Plus, if you remember, my wheelchair won't get around there, and you know it. They don't think of people like me and the access I need. You're doing this on purpose. You resent me and want to make me feel bad for my disability. Well, I won't do it. It's unfair."

"Then what do you suggest we do?"

Sally was silent. She sat in her chair, hands flexing as she looked at the cluster of stalls in the distance. "It's not up to me. You're the able-bodied one. I can't do everything, you know."

"We need food. Water. Maybe we can barter with someone down there."

"With what? We don't have anything. Besides, I need your attention, not those people. I'm family. It's not my fault I can't help myself. You owe me."

Delia tuned out the sound of her sister's whining and went on, pushing the wheelchair ahead of her. She focussed her energy on the squeaking wheel, keeping that at the forefront of her mind so she didn't have to listen to the never-ending self-pity and moaning from her younger sibling. Hate was a strong word, and one she didn't quite have the ability to justify feeling towards her. She supposed the nearest she could think of to explain how she felt was burdened. Existing alone in the world was hard enough. Caring for her sister and her demanding nature made it almost impossible.

***

The market was ramshackle at best. Tattered stores selling foraged goods were arranged in a rough circle for the wanderers who happened to pass on the road. Sally was right. It wasn't wheelchair friendly. People glared at them as they tried to inch their way through the crowds of people trying to beg and swap items.

"I told you we shouldn't have come here. You've done this on purpose to embarrass me because I'm in a wheelchair, haven't you? It's not fair. You hate me," Sally moaned.

Delia ignored her and concentrated on not running into anyone. She saw the wood ramp she had been looking for and made for it, pushing the wheelchair up it onto the raised stage.

"What are you doing? Where are you taking me?"

Delia pushed the chair into the centre of the stage, flicked on the brakes, then stood beside her sister, looking out into the eager crowd.

A man joined them. He was filthy, his hair in greasy knots, beard thick and salty. He looked from sister to sister then handed Delia a bag. She looked inside. Six bottles of water. Some bread and cheese. Discreetly tucked away at the side, a handgun and two boxes of ammunition.

"Just like we agreed last week, if you still want to go through with it" the man said, holding Delia's gaze.

"What's going on, why are we here? Everyone is staring at me. Take me down from here right now," Sally said, glaring at her sister.

Delia paid her no attention. She closed the drawstring on the tatty canvas bag and slung it over her shoulder. "This looks right. The deal stands," she said, locking eyes with the man.

The man smiled and put a hand on Sally's shoulder.

"Get off me, this man is touching me. Delia, tell him to stop. Tell him he can't do this to me, I'm disabled."

Delia tuned her sister out and locked eyes with the man. She thought this part would be hard, or at least cause some kind of conflict within her that would force her to change her mind, but her heart had grown cold like the world, and any love that once existed for her sister had perished some time ago. She turned, adjusted the weight of the bag on her shoulder and then exited the way she had come, heading down the ramp towards the crowd.

Sally saw her go and started to call after her. "Wait, where are you going? You can't just leave me here with these people. I'm disabled, it's your job to look after me. Delia? Delia? Can you hear me? Come back here."

Delia paused and looked over her shoulder. For a brief moment, she locked eyes with her sister, then glanced at the awning above the stage.

The words 'Meat Auction' were penned in unsteady hand on a banner pinned to the top of the framework. She glanced at the man who had given her the bag, nodded, then turned away as he started to take bids for their latest fresh delivery. Soon enough, Sally's cries were lost to Delia as she pushed her way through the crowd. She felt no shame, no sadness, only a sense of relief and for the first time optimism that the road ahead might not be quite so challenging anymore. She disappeared into the night, another anonymous face with a guilty secret trying to make the best she could of the situation. At last, she felt as if she was finally free.

CHAPTER FIVE

The world was slow to come into focus, the memories of his ordeal for the time being, unremembered. He blinked, taking in his surroundings. He was in a room, the paint on the ceiling faded and chipped. Slowly, his senses came back to him, but he didn't move. He lay perfectly still, trying to sense and feel his environment and piece together what had happened to him. He was in a bed, an actual real bed, the material soft under his body, itchy cover pulled up to his chin. He slowly moved his head, taking in more of the room. Basic furnishings. A tired dresser. A tatty armchair in the corner, chunks of foam missing from the arms. A window, the world nothing but a square of grey sky from his vantage point. A door. Warped, the blue paint cracked. He listened, holding his breath, trying to piece together how he got there, where he even was. He could hear muffled voices, but couldn't place where they were coming from. He tried to move, the bed creaking in protest as he touched his head. He felt bandages instead of the gash which he expected to be there, which added to his confusion. He could remember the old man in the church, McCarthy. He could remember being captured and put in the cage. He remembered planning to escape, to attack one of the brothers when the chance arose, and then…nothing. Everything was blank. He knew he had been injured in some way, but the details were still hazy.

For a sickening moment, he thought he was back there, that he had fainted before he got too far away and they had come back for him. That, however, didn't seem right. They were all about bars and cages, not beds and bandages. He sat up and swung his legs out of the bed, waiting for the dizziness to pass. He stood and staggered to the window. Outside was a faded wooden building, the side filling his entire field of vision.

"You're awake then."

He spun towards the voice, another surge of nausea almost making him topple to the ground.

"Easy, take a breath," the woman said from the door, keeping a close eye on him. Like most people, she was ageless. In a world without makeup, or hair products, everyone had the same dishevelled, grimy look to them. She had short, greasy hair which was dirty blonde and streaked with grey. One eye was milky white and stared sightlessly at him. The other was brown and regarded him with caution.

"How did I get here?" he asked.

"We found you a few miles from here. We almost left you there assuming you were dead until you happened to move. Lucky for you, or you would have died there."

"Where am I?"

"Somewhere safe," she said, keeping her distance. "That cut on your head was pretty ugly. Looks like you might have a fractured skull too. Lucky for you, we had people here who can help."

"What kind of people?" he asked, recalling his experiences with McCarthy.

"*Good* people. People who are trying to rebuild something from what we have left."

He looked around the room, panic setting in. "My bag, my things…"

"Over there in the corner. Nobody has touched them. That I promise you."

He went to it, opening it and checking that his things were in there, fragments of lives from a dead world, not quite sure why he was so protective over them. The woman watched from the entrance to the door.

"You got a name?" she asked.

The Collector glanced at her and shrugged. "I don't know. Nobody ever gave me one that I remember."

"So what do people call you?"

He thought about it, shrugged, then sat on the edge of the bed. "I don't really talk to people long enough to get to the names part. I suppose I just don't have one. I call myself the Collector, I suppose, if I have to use something."

"That's no good," she said, smiling at him. "Names are what makes us human. Without a name, you might as well just be dead."

"Do you have a name?" he asked.

"I do. My name is Betty."

He grunted and nodded, then sat on the end of the bed, unsure what to do next.

"We can't introduce you to the others if you don't have a name. How about we give you one now?"

He looked at her, overcome with emotion he thought had long been burned out of him by the daily grind of existence. "You'd do that? Give me a name?"

"We don't have any right to do that, as it's not ours to give."

"Oh."

"But I can help *you* choose a name. Something people can call you. It might seem like a little thing, but it makes all the difference. All it comes down to is choosing the right one."

She thought for a moment, folding her arms and leaning on the doorframe. "Let's see, what were your parents called?"

He shook his head. "I don't remember them."

"Alright, then where are you from, which city?"

He looked at her, blank and embarrassed. "I don't know. I don't remember ever coming from anywhere. I just…was."

"Are there any names you like?" she asked, keeping calm and

patient.

"I don't really know any."

"Alright, wait here. I have something that might help."

She left him. He listened to her feet echo on tired floorboards, then a door opening down the hall. A few minutes later, she came back and held out a book, its front faded, spine frayed, pages yellowed. On the front was a picture of a child. The title of the book read: 101 Baby Names for Boys and Girls, Second Edition. He took it and looked at the picture.

"Baby names?" he said, glancing at her.

"Just names. Babies grow up into adults. That thing's been hanging around here since before we arrived. Lucky for you, we didn't throw it out."

He opened the book, the pages brittle with age and giving off the distinct smell only old, well-thumbed paper gave. He started to read.

"Those are the girls' names. Move on closer to the middle," Betty said, coming into the room and sitting on the bed beside him. He did as she said, moving to the middle of the book and to the long list of boys' names. He smiled, never imagining he would ever get to choose what he would be called.

"Abraham. I like that," he said, glancing at her.

"Well, that's just the start. Keep looking. Choose one that really sings to you."

"Sings to me?" he said, frowning.

"Not actually sings, but…you'll know the one when you see it. Just take your time."

He looked at the lists, considering each name in turn. "This one," he said, pointing to one. "I like this one."

Betty leaned over and looked at where he was pointing. "Ethan? I like it. Good choice."

He smiled and handed her back the book. "Thank you…I've

never had a name before."

"You have, you just don't remember it. From now on you are Ethan. That's all that matters."

"Ethan," he repeated. It felt strange to say it. He grinned.

"Do you feel up to a walk? I can show you around the place. Introduce you to some of the others."

He nodded. "Yeah, I think so."

"You can leave your bag here if you like, or you can take it with you. It's up to you."

"No, I'll leave it here," he said. He trusted Betty. Although the experiences with McCarthy were still fresh in his mind, he felt he could trust her. For the time being at least. Besides, she had already helped him more than anyone else he had ever met in his life had bothered to do. He reminded himself that not everyone in the world could be bad, and that somewhere, good people still existed. He stood and stretched. Betty walked to the door, then turned back to him.

"Come on then, let me show you around the place."

He exited the room and followed her as she walked down a hallway, the floorboards bare and dusty, walls a pale blue. There were other doors spaced evenly down one side. The other was windowless.

"What is this place?" he asked as they walked slowly down the hall.

"It used to be a school building. Now it's where we sleep. There are only twelve of us here in the town right now, but it's enough for us to get by."

Ethan nodded, trying to shoo away memories of the way McCarthy had tried to lure him into feeling safe. They reached some steps and descended together, old wood creaking underfoot.

"We've been here for about two years now. Existing. Getting by. We don't look for trouble and so far none has found us."

She stopped on the steps and looked at him, one good eye penetrating into his. "You're not trouble are you, Ethan?"

He shook his head, shocked by the directness of the question.

"No, I didn't think so. I just wanted to ask you outright. Even with one eye, I can spot a lie pretty easily. I believe you."

She went on, leading the way. They came out into a larger room that looked like it was once a hall of some kind. Tables were set up in a makeshift dining area. Beyond that, a rudimentary kitchen area.

"This is where we spend most of our nights. It's not much, but it's warm and dry. We make the best of it."

Ethan looked at it. He could imagine it filled with people, friendly people who wouldn't try to eat him or fatten him up.

"What do you do for food?" he asked.

"We fish."

"Fish?" he repeated, then stopped and stared at her. "You've seen the ocean?"

"Of course. Haven't you?"

"Never. It's what I was trying to find when this happened." He pointed to the bandage on his head.

She smiled at him. "Come with me," she said, walking across the hall. At the end were two double doors. She stopped at them and turned back to him. "This could be your lucky day."

She pushed open the doors, letting the diffused daylight pour in. Ethan blinked and stepped outside, letting his eyes adjust to the gloom. For a moment, he couldn't breathe, his eyes unbelieving of the things they were seeing.

The schoolhouse was on a hill, a scattering of other buildings below it. All of them the same, faded wood, tired paint. People were moving around, going about their daily business. At the bottom of the hill was a dock, and beyond it, the ocean, stretching out into the distance as far as he could see. It wasn't blue like in

81

the postcard, it was a dull grey and dirty, but to see it there, an undulating mass of endless waves, filled him with a light giddiness he had never experienced before. He exhaled, realising he had forgotten to breathe. He stared at the water, realising that it was, without question, the most beautiful thing he had ever seen. He blinked and felt tears on his cheeks. He didn't care. Nothing could spoil his perfect moment.

"Are you okay?" Betty asked.

He nodded. "It's just…I didn't expect…" The words wouldn't come in any sort of sense. They were jumbled and incoherent even to him. All he could think about was the beauty of the ocean. It dawned on him that even though the world had been left a dying, ugly place of such wretched hopelessness, there was still some beauty left in it.

"Do you need a minute?" Betty asked.

"No, no, I'm okay, it's just…It's so beautiful."

She looked at him, then at the water. "If you say so. To me, it's nothing unusual. It's where we get our food, that's all."

"You fish from the dock?"

"Not exactly. There's time to go into that later."

"Can I go take a closer look at it?" he asked.

"At the water?"

He nodded, unable to take his eyes from the undulating waves.

"Of course, you go take a look. I'll tell the others you're awake."

They walked down the hill together, the dirt path winding around the shells of buildings that remained. As they neared the foot of the hill, Betty veered off towards a group of people who were watching from a distance, paying particular attention to Ethan. He barely noticed them. He walked to the dock, trembling as he got closer. He could hear it now, the ebb and flow of the water. He hoped it would look clearer as he approached, but it was just as dirty as it had appeared from the schoolhouse. He looked out at it, blinking back the sudden wetness in his eyes, then he fell to his knees and wept.

TWO

He was summoned to a meeting. They took him to a long hall with high shadow-covered ceilings. A rough table sat at one end behind which five people sat. He stood before them, hands clasped in front of him, feeling their eyes on him. Candles flickered in the corners of the room, giving it an ethereal, almost dream-like feel. Of the four who were seated, three he didn't recognise. The three were men, two of them old and grizzled, eyes pale and mistrustful, they could have been related, such was the similarity of their appearance. The other man was younger. He looked like he had at one time been overweight, and although the harsh environment had caused him to shed the excess, he didn't carry it well, several large folds of skin hanging loose on his jowls and neck. He had a thick beard, and his massive hands were folded on the table. With them was Betty. She stood and watched him carefully.

"How are you feeling?" the bearded man asked.

"Better, thanks."

"Ethan, isn't it?"

He nodded, flicking his eyes towards Betty. "Yes."

"My name is Barnes. This is John Mannering." He pointed to the first of the two men to his right. Mannering nodded, his face betraying no emotion.

"Next to him is Roy Glover. Despite what you may think, they are unrelated. They just happen to look alike," Barnes said. "Of course, you already know Betty. She tells us you're a good man, which is why we brought you here today."

Ethan looked around the hall, then at Barnes. "This place you have here…"

"It's functional," Barnes said. "We work together and eke out a decent existence for ourselves. We stay out of trouble when we can and keep to ourselves."

"That don't mean we can't look after ourselves if things get ugly," Glover said.

Barnes glanced at the older man and smiled, showing the gap where his front teeth should have been. "You'll have to excuse Roy, his manners aren't what they used to be."

"I'm not here to cause trouble," Ethan said. "I just wanted to see the sea."

Mannering snorted down his nose and glanced at Barnes.

"Something wrong?" Ethan asked.

"No, not at all. John, like all of us, is just wary of strangers, that's all," Barnes said

"You don't have to worry. I'm not here to cause trouble."

"You had a pretty nasty injury when we found you. Looks like trouble found you easily enough."

"It did, but that wasn't my fault. I trusted someone I shouldn't have and…" He cleared his throat and lowered his eyes to the dusty floorboards. "I made a mistake and almost died for it."

"Do you want to tell us about it?" Barnes asked.

Ethan didn't know it if was some kind of trick question and shrugged his shoulders. "Not really. Like I said, I made a mistake."

"Which is why we brought you here tonight. We can't afford mistakes, not now. We're building something out of the ashes of what went before. We have to be very particular about who we allow to stay with us," Barnes replied. He was clearly the man in charge, and everyone seemed to respect him.

"I'm not looking for a free ride. I can help you, I can work,"

Ethan said.

"What do you do?" Mannering asked.

"Anything. Whatever you ask. I just…I like it here. By the ocean, by the water. It's…beautiful."

Mannering looked at him, eyes glassy with uncertainty. "You pulling my chain, boy?"

"Sorry?" Ethan said.

"Easy, John, give him a break. He's new around here. Try to keep that in mind."

"Look, I don't understand what you want from me," Ethan said, glancing at them in turn. "I didn't walk in here looking for help. You found me and brought me here, which I'm thankful for, you helped, me, bandaged me up, I just…I've spent so much time alone I don't really know what you want me to say."

"We just want to know about you," Barnes replied. "Who you are, where you came from. How you survived. That's the main thing."

"What do you mean?"

"Well, there's a right way to survive, and a wrong way to survive. We only want people here who are interested in surviving the right way. If you went down that other route, then I don't think there's a future here for you."

"So what do you want to know exactly?"

"Like I said, who are you? Where did you come from and how did you survive?"

They were all things that Ethan had no answers to. He wasn't sure if what he was about to say were right or wrong, or the answers Barnes was even looking for, but he decided honesty was best, and that they would either accept it or they wouldn't. If they did, he would see how things went. If they didn't, then he would carry on walking, maybe follow the coastline and see how far it went. He quite liked that idea. It appealed to him. He realised they were waiting for an answer and cleared his throat.

"I don't remember the world before. I've heard about it, of course, like everyone. Rumours, stories. I don't know which ones were true and which ones weren't. The truth of it is, it doesn't matter. For me, this is all it's ever been. As for who I am and what my place is, I don't have the answer to that either. I wake up each day knowing it could be my last, that just one infection, one illness, one bad encounter on the road would mean it's over for me. I know nobody would miss me, and I know I have no reason to expect otherwise. I've drifted around looking for a place to call my own, looking for a purpose. You people, this place, it's the first time I've seen something that seems to be building something instead of just waiting to die. I've done things I'm not proud of, and I've seen things that make me wonder what the point of this existence even is, but I don't have answers to that either. All I can tell you is that I try to do the right thing and make sure I make it through another day. I can't do any more than that. I'm not sure if that's the answer any of you were looking for, but that's the truth."

Barnes folded his hands and leaned across the table. "Everyone here has a purpose. A reason for being here. We all have jobs. We don't freeload. You understand that, right?"

"I said I'm willing to help. I'll do anything you want me to if it means I can stay for a while. Maybe this won't work out for any of us, in which case I'll be on my way and look elsewhere for whatever it is I'm trying to find."

Mannering leaned across and whispered something in Barnes's ear. Ethan watched as Barnes nodded. "You said you like the water. You also look strong. Have you ever been on a boat before?"

He shook his head. "No. I've never even seen the ocean before."

Barnes turned to Mannering. "We could use him on the next trip. Especially with what happened to Chris."

"No, he's not ready for that. He couldn't handle it."

"I can handle it, whatever it is," Ethan cut in.

Mannering glared at him. "I wasn't talking to you, I was talking to my friend here."

"Maybe he can handle it," Barnes said, then turned back to Mannering. "We definitely need a third hand out there."

"We do, but not him. He would break out there."

"I wouldn't," Ethan cut in again, earning another glare from Mannering.

Barnes grinned and looked down the table to Betty. "He's keen, isn't he?"

Betty grinned, Mannering looked ready to explode.

"Alright," Barnes said. "You can stay for a while. You'll be expected to come out and fish with us. If you want to earn your keep, that's how you'll do it."

"This is crazy, look at him," Mannering said. "He can't go out there like that with a broken skull."

Barnes nodded, then looked Ethan in the eye, his gaze unwavering. "Let him heal first. He's no good to anyone with that wound the way it is anyway."

"You mean I can stay?" Ethan asked.

"On a trial basis. Until we decide what to do. Be aware; we'll be watching you. If at any point you do anything that we don't like, you'll be out of here. Understood?"

Ethan nodded. "Understood. I won't let you down."

"Alright," Barnes replied. "Now go get some rest. Sooner you're fit, the sooner we can find something for you to do around here."

"Just one more thing," Ethan asked.

"Go on."

He looked at Mannering, resisting the urge to turn away from his glare. "What is it like out there on the water?"

Mannering glanced at Barnes, looked like he was about to speak, then changed his mind. Instead, he smirked and folded his massive arms. "Ask me again in a couple of weeks. Maybe then I'll tell you something about it."

Ethan frowned, but didn't want to do anything to jeopardize his chances of staying.

"Alright," Barnes cut in, chair scraping across the wood floor as he stood up. "I think we're done here. Rest for a few days, then we'll talk again. Until that time, maybe keep a low profile around here. People are weary of strangers. Until they know and trust you, don't be surprised if they don't seem particularly welcoming. If you stick with it though, they'll come around. I have a pretty good sense of character, and I think you'll turn out just fine."

"I will, and thank you. You won't regret this."

"You might," Mannering grunted as he too stood.

"Don't start, John," Betty said as she crossed the room to stand beside Ethan. She looked at him. The one friendly face he had seen.

"Don't tell me not to start, I'm the only voice of reason here it seems."

"We need all the help we can get."

"Not from just anyone you find lying out there in the dirt."

"This enough, both of you," Barnes said, raising his voice enough to stop the argument.

"Come on, you need some rest. Maybe some food too," Betty said to Ethan, leading him out of the hall.

"I have some with me. Just beans but…"

"It's fine. We have plenty of food to go around. Come on, I'll show you around the village. Despite what these two are saying, there are some nice people here."

THREE

For the next week, Ethan did his best to integrate with the people of the town. Some were open to him and kind, others still approached him with mistrust. Betty had allowed him to stay in the room where he had been taken after they found him, and for the first time, Ethan felt no desire to go in search of something else. He had everything he wanted. The town setup was basic, but functional. There was a real sense of positivity about the people, and they had food and water, the latter somehow purified to remove much of the sulphur, ash taste. As suggested by Barnes, he had kept a low profile, keeping mostly to himself and interacting only with Betty, who changed his bandages every second day. She told him she had put eleven stitches in his skin, and in between bandage changes, he had looked in the dirty dresser mirror at the ugly cut. It would leave a scar, but he was fine with that. The alternative at the time was something he was unwilling to think about. He had also, for the first time, cut his hair and shaved his beard, which took years off him. His eyes were still old and told the story of the toil of his existence, but the clean shave had taken fifteen years off his appearance. He looked like a stranger. Square jaw, defined cheekbones. The new look made him more approachable around town, people started to come and talk to him, dropping their guards slightly. One thing that didn't change was Ethan's love for the ocean. To him, it was still beautiful, and he woke early most mornings and went to the dock, where he would sit with his feet hanging over the side and just look at it, the way it rippled and moved. He wished he would have been able to see it when it was still blue. It was one such morning when Mannering spoke to him for the first time since the meeting he had attended.

"You still here?" he barked.

Ethan looked over his shoulder. Mannering was standing there, arms folded, tatty red-and-black-checkered shirt flapping in the breeze.

"I am. My head is almost healed. I'm almost ready to start work."

"I was hoping you might have decided to move on," Mannering slurred. Although it was early, he was drunk. Ethan could smell it on him when the wind blew.

"No, I'm still here and happy to find my place."

"It's stupid, you should just go and leave us alone here."

Ethan stood, facing Mannering who was unsteady on his feet.

"Isn't it a bit early to be drinking?"

"I've only had one, for the cold. Anyway, I need it. Fishing trip in a few days. They want you to come. I'm fighting them on it though, I don't want you out there."

"What's your problem with me, Mannering? You've hated me ever since I showed up. I'm not a bad person."

Mannering staggered closer, bringing the smell of booze with him. "I don't hate you, I just don't have time to babysit stupid kids out there. You don't get it, you don't know what it's like."

"I've heard the stories about what might be out there," Ethan said, glancing to the ocean. "Big things. Dangerous things."

Mannering shook his head. "Not stories. You people never learn until it's too late."

"I don't understand what you're problem is with me."

"It's not just you," Mannering snapped. "It's all of you. Twelve men were lost out there fishing. Twelve lost, more injured because, like you, they thought they knew best. You don't know a damn thing."

"Maybe if you didn't drink so much it would be safer out there."

Mannering lurched forward, stopping inches from Ethan's face. "You don't get it. This isn't about stories or things you've heard. I've been out there. I've seen what's in the water. You don't seem to see anything past how nice the water looks. That's going to get you killed out there."

"I don't –"

"Shut up," Mannering snapped. "Betty tells me you like to read. To collect things from other people's lives."

"Yeah, I do. What does that have to do with anything?"

Mannering stepped back and pulled a small red book out of his pocket. "Read this. I found it on the boat we use to fish. We had to tow the boat in, but we were able to repair it. You think it's just stories, but it's more real than you could ever imagine. You sit yourself down and you read that. Maybe then you'll change your mind about playing fisherman." Mannering shoved the book into Ethan's hand. He looked at it, then back at Mannering to question what was happening, but Mannering was already staggering back up the dock towards the village. Ethan looked again at the book, and with Mannering's words fresh in his head, sat on the edge of the dock again. He started to read.

INTERLUDE FIVE
GONE FISHING

July 7th

I can't remember the sun.

Some of the old timers claim to recall it, but the world I know has always been this shade of grey. The rains come often, but they are more ash than water, and leave a greasy sheen on the skin. People around here call me James, and although I know it's not my real name, I don't argue. Names don't matter. What matters is that I – we – are still here. The last survivors of a dead world. I have dated the start of this journal as July 7th just for the sake of keeping records, although the truth is, we stopped counting days and months long ago after the event. If nothing else, it will serve to keep my thoughts in order as I write them down.

The story of what happened isn't one that any of us like to talk about. After all, we all lived it. We know. We look into each other's eyes and there is something there. Shared knowledge, shared respect. I don't really know what it is. Some kind of solidarity. It's funny, because in the movies back before the world actually went and died on us, they always painted a picture of scattered groups of mangy survivors hiding from cannibalistic bandits and trying to make their way to salvation. The reality is that there are no bandits, not that I know of at least. In fact, those of us who are left have pulled together. I don't know if it's good fortune or irony that it took the world going to hell around us to finally make us set aside petty squabbles and come together to survive. Our group consists of seven people. We had twelve until recently, but we lost two on our last hunt, and another four to cancer.

Damn radiation, that's the enemy now. Even as we struggle to survive, it eats away at us. That and the things in the water.

Before I get to that, I think a little backstory is in order. I managed to find this journal in the ruins of a schoolhouse, and borrowed a pen from Gimmy, who, out of everyone, understands best why I need to get this on paper. See, I'm pretty sure I'm dying. The cough that started a few weeks ago is getting worse and I have started to bring up blood. My nails and hair haven't started to fall out yet, but I don't think it will be too long before it happens.

Brad thought I was just paranoid when I told him I thought I was on my way out, but he can't understand that I can feel it inside. It's in there, mutating my cells, screwing around with my internal composition, rearranging the furniture.

The others don't seem too concerned about my plight. We have all become desensitised to death, and even though they don't say it, the look in their eyes tells me they see me as a dead man walking – an inconvenience; an extra mouth to feed when food is scarce. They won't cut me loose from the group, but I don't think many tears will be shed when I join the other four billion plus who have died on this god-forsaken ball of rock since this all began.

We go hunting in a few days, and that means facing those things. Brad thinks they are stupid and mindless, but I don't think so. They know we can't live off the land, and that our only food source is out there with them. I keep wanting to call them fish, but that would be an understatement.

They are mutations, things that used to live in the oceans and ruined by the event that killed the planet. I'm scared, and to think about it too much scares me to the point where I'm not sure I want to write it down. I don't have time to go into it now anyway, so I'll step back and give it some thought. The shadows are getting longer, and we will have to get the fire going soon. The nights are so cold. Tomorrow, I'll tell you all about how this thing started.

July 8th

Didn't sleep too well. This damn cough kept me awake, and the few times I did drift off, I dreamed of those things out in the water. For as much as we have coped with a lot, it's hard to handle how they look. First one I saw was twenty footer. Imagine a whale mingled with a squid and then turned half inside out, and you would be somewhere in the right ballpark. They are hellish, violent things, their need to hunt us as much as we them, making our clashes inevitable. But all that will be told in time. Later today, we go out to face them, and that frightens me more than I could ever express in words.

The day of the event was a Thursday. Nobody knows for sure what it was. Different people hear different things. Weapons test gone wrong, solar storm, polar shift, hell, even an act of God. The best explanation I heard for it was an asteroid. A guy I met said he's heard all about it from someone who saw it go down (I'm not sure someone so close to such a devastating event would survive, but we have to take everything with a pinch of salt these days). According to him, the man said it cut through the sky at over 20,000 miles per hour, and impacted somewhere in the Pacific Ocean. The sky lit up, and then the world became shrouded in darkness – a worldwide blanket of ash which blotted out the sun. Millions were killed by the blast and the resulting tidal surges; countless others by the fallout. Nothing was left untouched. Nothing escaped the hell that came. That, at least, was his story. Someone else told me it was a white flash, a high-pitched sound and then things started to die. Trees, people, animals. The fact is, nobody knows for sure what it was or how it happened, but the end result is the same. You know, it's funny, in a way. For all the arrogance of man, it astounds me just how quickly we died out as a species. There was no fight, no master plan. Nature simply decided our time was done and wiped us out. I wish I had more answers for you, but the truth is I don't. The world is how it is and nobody knows for sure why or what happened. That's all I can tell you. It might have been better if everyone had died, but the human race is nothing if not strong; or maybe it's unlucky. Either way, there are a few of us left. Mostly we're skeletal, filthy wretches with haunted eyes that only tell part of the horror of what we've experienced.

I sit now in this abandoned husk of a building, its interior as ravaged and barren as we all feel inside. Some of the others question why I bother to write something down when there is no hope that anybody will ever read it, and I suppose they have a point. I think whatever my reasons, it makes me feel better to get it down on paper. Maybe, just maybe, whoever you are that might be reading this, are in a better world than this one.

I think about what is about to take place, about going out on the water, and it fills me with a horror even worse than the lingering stench of ash and death that clings to those of us who are left. Benson just told me that he understands if I don't want to go out there with them, mumbling something about my condition. I know he didn't mean to cause offence, but I still found myself getting defensive, screaming and shouting that I was fine. Truth is, I don't want to go out there, but to stay here would be to admit that I'm dying, and I don't want that either. None of us would be going out there if we didn't have to. Let them keep the damn oceans to themselves if that's what they want, but the fact is, we have no choice. They are the only thing left that we can eat, and so we have no choice but to hunt them. Even though they gave me a readymade excuse not to go, I still have my pride and want to prove my worth out there before I find a quiet corner to die in. I need to get away from these people, at least for a while. It's funny that even in a world as empty as this one, we still need to spend time by ourselves.

July 9th

Had to get away yesterday. Hated looking at their faces. They look at me like I'm some kind of leper. I suppose in a way I am. I walked out into the bleak wastes, everything covered in grey ash or burned and broken. Bodies of the dead lie mummified in their thousands, some taking on a ghostly stone effect from the ash build up. It reminded me of something from Pompeii, and I almost laughed outright. The quiet is something that I still struggle to get used to. There is absolute deathly silence. There are no birds left to sing, no animals left to scratch at the undergrowth. No people to exchange nods with and share pleasantries. More and more often I wonder about my wife and daughter and I ask myself for the millionth time if it's possible they somehow survived. I know, of course, that they didn't. I went to all the places where I knew they would go if we were separated and found nothing but death and destruction. I only hope for them it was quick and painless. I wouldn't wish this life I have now on anybody.

July 10th

Barely slept last night. I think it was because I know today is the day that we head out onto the water. Even Stan was tense this morning as he checked the netting and harpoon guns. Four of us are going out. There is me (obviously), and Benson, who once again told me he understood if I didn't want to go. He's a nice guy and he means well, but I'm not about to be seen as a coward. Also coming with us is Toby. He's pretty new to the group. Found him wandering down the side of the road, weaving around burned-out husks of cars. He's only fifteen, and although he talks like the big man, this morning I saw fear in his eyes. The kid shouldn't be ashamed. We all feel it. It's like a physical thing, hanging in the air with the ash and the smell of rot and death. Benson told him not to worry, and that he was going out there as a boy, but coming back as a man. I don't believe that. After all, I've seen what's out there. In charge of the fishing trip is Stan. He knows all about these things and claims to have caught dozens of them before he joined up with our group. He certainly talks the talk, and we couldn't help but feel reassured as he told us exactly how it will go down out there. He says there is a spot around eighty miles off the coast where these creatures roam, and that will be our best bet of finding them.

It sounds crazy I'm sure. Hell, it looks crazy even writing it down. Nobody in their right minds would go looking for these things, but we are all hungry and have people relying on us. If we could manage to snag one, even one of the smaller ones, it would give us food for a few days. We would be able to eke out another few weeks of existence. Of course we all know the dangers. There is a reason going out there is a last resort. We know before we even set off that we might never come back. From where I sit, perched on the hood of a burned-out car, I can see the ocean. It laps against the shore. In the water are the rusting remains of a passenger plane, it's blue and white frame a flashback to a life which is long dead. I look at the water, a dark undulating mass, and I know that they are out there. It's starting to rain, and I need to get to shelter. The last thing I want to happen now is to catch a cold. I'll be back soon to write some more.

We are on our way. It's still raining, so we are all cramped together here in the galley (no food, of course!). Nobody is talking too much. I think we are all just trying to deal with what we are about to do in our own special way. The boat is a ninety-foot crabber. It has seen better days, but is still seaworthy. Not many boats survived after the impact, so to find one still useable was something of a miracle. A minor victory in our hellish life, and the reason why we have set up camp by the water. Like our ancestors, we live near our food source, although this is quite unlike anything our ancestors had to deal with. The gentle rise and fall of the bow is making me sleepy, and I might even think I could get a couple of hours sleep if not for the nervous excitement of our situation. My stomach feels like a tight ball, and the nerves are really starting to kick in as the safety of land gets lost in the ash-filled sleety haze.

The kid, Toby, looks terrified. He seems to have left his usual bravado on the shore, and he looks every bit the frightened child that he is. Hell, I can't blame him. We are all scared, apart from Stan. He's maybe in his forties, his hair long and silver, just like his beard. It's his eyes that concern me though. There is a little bit of craziness in them. A little glint of something not quite right.

This, incidentally, is my second fishing trip. The first one was a few weeks ago. We managed to catch a fifteen footer. It looked like an overgrown, deformed eel. We fought for hours to wrestle it on board and kill it. It writhed and thrashed on the deck, and I still don't know how we managed to kill it without anyone getting injured. Oh, I should mention something else too. My hair is starting to fall out. I'm pretty sure that means I definitely have radiation sickness. It shouldn't be a surprise, not really, but it's still a shock. I think I'm going to go stretch my legs out on deck. Maybe I'll try to talk to the kid and see if I can get him to relax a little. God knows, he looks like he needs it.

Benson thought he saw one of them breach the surface.

We stopped the boat and stared out into the water. It was eerie, an absolute flat calm. The silence was thick and we were grateful for the wind which rocked the boat as it drifted on the tide. We stared at the water for a while, half hoping that it was what we were looking for, half not. Something spooked the old man alright. You can see it in his eyes. As usual, only Stan seems unafraid. We might have stood there all day had he not started the engines again and set off on our way. We seem to be further out than usual. I asked Stan where we were headed and he mumbled something about deeper waters.

That scares me.

We all know that the deeper the water, the bigger these things are. Some people claim they grow to hundreds of feet in length. Some side effect of the event. Nobody I know has ever seen one that big. Stan said he saw fifty footer once, and that for me is plenty big enough. I tried talking to the kid, but whenever I try to get through to him, he throws his guard up. It's almost like if he doesn't admit that he is scared, he won't come to any harm. That's not a bad outlook to have I suppose, but the downside is it will hit him really hard when we finally make contact.

One thing I should point out which might be a sore subject when you come to read this. Just know that (hopefully) the world is a much better and less desperate time for you than it is for us now. Maybe for you, bait shops exist, as do other things to lure in our predators. For us, we have no such luxury, so we have to make use of what we have. The key is to find a body that still has plenty of meat on them. They don't seem to mind so much about the rot, as long as they are meaty. I know they were once people, but this isn't a time where we can afford to be picky. Besides, we have to do something to draw them to us. Anyway, you can save your judgement. We do what we have to in order to survive. End of story.

God, I'm hungry. That's the plus side of food being so scarce. We can't afford to be picky. Believe me, I have wondered on more than once occasion if we are doing more harm than good by eating stuff that swims in these polluted seas, but then I also remind myself that we don't really have much of a choice. It's like the way a bear might chew through its own paw to escape a trap. Sometimes, you just have to do whatever you have to in order to survive.

We are definitely going further out than usual. I hope Stan knows what he's doing.

I intended to do this sooner, but my hands were shaking too badly. We saw…something. The right words for what it was are too hard to find right now. All I know is that it was big, almost beyond my ability to comprehend. I'm not exaggerating here, when I tell you that it was at least two hundred feet, or at least the part of it that we could see was. It's back arched out of the water, and it was a mottled pinky brown. There was a half-developed tentacle growing out of it, squirming and thrashing as the misplaced appendage broke the surface of the water. It was as thick as the oak tree that used to be in our backyard when I was a kid, a memory that until I saw that hellish creature, I had completely forgotten about.

The kid is crying. He's trying to be quiet, but we can all hear it. The fact that nobody is trying to help him or offer comfort says a lot about the current mind-set of those of us who are left. We are living all of those clichés of old. It's a dog-eat-dog world, only the strong survive etc. etc.

Don't get me wrong, I would love to help him. As I peek over the top of the pad as a write this, I can see him on the seat opposite me. Knees pulled up to his chin, head down as the boat crests the waves in pursuit of our creature. I think he would take that now, that comfort or reassurance. The simple fact is that I have none to give. I have my own problems, my own issues and my own fears, the most pressing of which is what we are going to do about our captain, who is now cackling and whistling as we chase this giant monster. Doesn't he know that we can't possibly hope to capture it? We're not experienced hunters or fishermen. Hell, we struggled to capture that fourteen-foot eel last time. What the hell does he expect us to do if we catch up to this thing? I look at the others, and they meet my gaze. We are all thinking the same thing, and wondering if we should do something or just wait and let things play out. Either way, I feel sick and just want to get back to dry land.

We have no business being out here.

#

Toby is dead, and I don't think the rest of us are too far behind.

I paused just after writing that and couldn't quite believe it. The poor kid lost it, panicked and charged at Stan, demanding we return to dry land. They got into a fight, although that's probably not the right word. Toby tried to attack Stan and got the hell beaten out of him for his troubles. Stan dragged the kid out on deck and straddled him, hitting him over and over again. The sound was so loud, so raw that I will never forget it. He eventually stopped fighting, but Stan carried on anyway. None of us moved, none of us even tried to help. I feel so guilty, but it still caused no reaction. Am I really that broken? Am I really so desensitised to this new world that I can't even find a reaction to a grown man beating a child to death while we all watch? Maybe this new earth is just what we deserve. We have become so barbaric that maybe death would have been too good for us.

#

We are under attack.
It keeps circling the boat.

#

Stan is quite mad. I'm sure of that now.
After he finished with Toby, Stan picked him up and tossed him over the side. He should have known how stupid that was. The fresh blood in the water must have been like a dinner bell, and that big thing we had been following turned its attention towards us.
We started to panic, but Stan just laughed.
If I live through this, I will never, ever forget how that thing looked as it came towards us.
What the hell do we do now?

#

Hahaha! You have to laugh. Not as dumb as they look these fish!!

#

Stan threw Benson over the side. He keeps looking at me and I think I might be next. Creature still circling. I feel like I should do something but I'm too afraid to move. I can feel his eyes on me, and when I glance up at them, I can see the crazy. I don't know if I'm more scared of him or this horrible thing that keeps circling us. Stan said as long as we keep feeding it, it should leave us alone, which is all well and good, but there is only me left. I get the feeling it's going to come down to him or me, and I don't think I can take him in a fair fight. Even if I could, what then?

This is all such a mess.

#

For all the worrying, I didn't even have to make the choice. Stan is gone, and now I'm alone. At least I am if you don't count our friend out there who is circling the boat. Some fishing trip hahahahaha!!! I feel like Captain Ahab, only I'm way out of my depth. This has to end soon, so I suppose I should explain what happened to Stan. I was trying to get him to return to land. There is no food or water on the boat, and it was this that I was trying to draw attention to, rather than the fact that he had killed two people since we came out here. He sat and listened, keeping those crazy eyes locked on me the entire time.

He heard me out, then told me that I knew what had to happen. That they had to be fed to make sure they are kept strong. He said it was so they could breed and make sure there was enough food to go around for everyone. He stood up then, and I was sure it was my time.

That's not what happened though. Stan had a knife, and he stabbed himself in the belly before he ran straight at the transom, screaming and cackling as he cut deeper and deeper. His knees hit the edge, and he tumbled over into the water, his screams cut off. I didn't watch the creature take him, but I heard it. Somehow, that was worse. I panicked then, because I was alone out there. I ran to the controls, not really knowing what I was doing. I managed to start the boat and had angled back to shore when I felt another nudge from underneath, then a shudder as the boat stopped moving. The engines were on, but my forward momentum had stopped. I had no drive, and I think I know what happened. It seems these animals aren't so dumb after all. It had destroyed the props and rudder, leaving me helpless. The perpetual grey dusk seems to be mocking me as my skeletal shadow stretches out across the deck. Out there on the water, it still circles. Every now and again, it will breach the surface, and I can see its milky eye as it watches me. Well, let it watch. I've decided to hunker down in here and wait for it to go away. I can be stubborn and patient if I want to, and this is one of those times where it will help me. Let it waste its energy out there if that's what it wants to do. I'm going to stay in here and keep you all entertained.

#

July 11??

Night came and went, and it's still out there. I didn't sleep much. Not because I didn't want to, believe me I'm exhausted, but that thing out there keeps nudging the boat. Not hard enough to damage it, but just enough to keep me afraid and on edge. The bastard is toying with me. I think it's the fear that is making me so tired. The night was a never-ending cycle of paranoia as I stared out of the window at the black waves. Even when it was too dark to see it, I could still hear it out there, breaching the surface and making its presence known.

Thoughts have turned to my own survival, and I really don't know what to do. As I may have already mentioned, there is no food on board. Worse than that though, there is no WATER.

How ironic that the stuff surrounds me but it's way too polluted to drink. Even if I could keep it down, it would kill me within hours. If I had some way to boil it, then maybe I would stand a chance, but I have nothing on me but this pad and pen I'm writing with. I suppose if things get desperate I can try to drink the ink haha!

In all seriousness though, I really am stuck here. It's not like I can just call the coastguard and wait for help to arrive. It just nudged the boat again. I think it's waiting for me, but I won't give up just yet. I shall just have to try and ignore the hunger and keep my thoughts on writing. I'm going to go and search the boat again and see if there is anything I might have missed.

#

Spent the last two hours going over every inch of the fishing boat. The creature has gone for now, but just when I start to relax and think I'm safe, it nudges the boat. I'm so tired. I really think I would feel better if it would just let me sleep. Either way, here is a list of exactly what I have on board here with me.

1 harpoon gun.
1 cigarette tin (Empty)
10 feet of fishing net
1 broken shard of mirror (I think it belonged to Toby)

1 putrid female corpse torso (for bait)
1 pad (on which I'm writing)
1 pen (with which I am writing this!!)

That's all. I don't see anything there that can help me out of this situation, and I'm starting to get scared. It's bad enough trying to get through the day as is, but stranded out here in such a confined space is hell. It's almost a form of sensory deprivation. The only sound is the creaking of the boat as it drifts in the tide and my guts grumbling for some kind of sustenance. Back at our camp, the others should have realised we are late back, not that they can do anything about it. I'm so tired. I might try to get my head down for a while.

#

Please, just let me sleep for a while. Just an hour is all I need.

#

July 12

Still no food or sleep. That fucking thing still keeps hitting the boat. I don't think I can take it anymore. I NEED food. What I wouldn't give for a nice cold glass of water. I don't want to write anymore. I need to think. Every hour that passes saps my energy.

#

13th

I think I heard my wife call to me in the night. I staggered out on deck, but I couldn't see her. And why would I? She's dead. Ha!

The thing is still circling the boat. Why won't it just leave me alone?

I'm so hungry.

14th

Couldn't help myself. It was meant for the fish, but it has eaten recently and I haven't ha!

The smell made me gag, but I forced myself to keep it down. The trick was to pretend it wasn't human.

What have I become?

15th July

Need to act now before it's too late. I never expected things to end this way. My wife is calling to me from somewhere down in the water, and I just want to be with her. I'm so thirsty, and at least that soon will be at an end. I hope I can bring myself to swallow enough water before that thing out there gets me. The thought of feeling those teeth puncture my skin while I'm still alive is one that frightens me almost to the point of backing out. But if I'm going to do this, then I intend to do it my own way. I intend to tie the harpoon to my leg with the fishing line. It should be heavy enough to make sure I sink.

This journal I shall leave here. I shall leave it by the controls. If by some miracle this boat remains afloat and you are reading this by the light of the sun, then I know at least that you are in a situation better than the world I am about to leave.

The creature is nudging the boat again. I only hope that if you are reading this that those creatures died with us who remained on this planet, and the world you inhabit is a safer, happier place.

It's time to go now. It's getting late, and I want to do this before I lose my nerve.

I hope this book finds you in good health. For me, it is time to go.

Tell them, if they ask where I am, that I have gone fishing.

James

CHAPTER SIX

There was little to differentiate light and day. When Ethan woke, he had no idea what time it was. Betty was standing by the door, a silhouette framed by the candlelight at her back.

"It's time to wake up. Big day today."

He grunted some form of response, then swung his legs out of the bed as she gently closed the door.

Since his arrival at the village he had been unable to think of anything but the journal. He had read it a dozen times; however, if Mannering's intention had been to frighten him off, it hadn't worked. He was curious, a fear-fuelled adrenaline surging through him. His integration with the village was going well, and he knew this was the next logical step in being accepted. This was a big day, his first day at work, his chance to contribute something and prove he was of some value. When he was dressed, he went downstairs. Betty had made him some food. He sat in front of the bowl of stew and began to eat as she sat opposite him. It was impossible to ignore the tension in her face.

They sat silent. He ate, she sat and watched him.

"Will you be careful out there?"

He looked up at her over his bowl. "I'll be fine. Nothing at all to worry about. I'm excited."

"It's dangerous out there on the water. I hoped they might give you work here on the land."

"I wanted to go out on the water. The idea of catching our food makes me happy. I'll have a purpose."

"I've heard terrible stories about the ocean. About creatures that live in it."

He stopped eating, steaming spoonful of soup hovering near

his mouth. "What kind of stories?" He thought of the journal Mannering had given him.

She averted her gaze. "It's not really for me to tell. I know it's dangerous out there though."

Ethan continued to eat, unable to tell her that her efforts to protect him were of no use. He already knew more than enough. "I'll be fine. I want to do this. I want to prove myself," he muttered.

"There are other ways to do that."

"I want to repay you for everything you've done. I want people to look at me like I'm worthy of being here."

"I know, I understand, I just…I want you to be careful. People here, for the most part, are already accepting of you. John Mannering isn't one of them, sure enough, but you don't need him to accept you. He's a bitter old drunk."

Unsure how to respond, he turned his attention back to his food. The stew was good and warmed him from within. He suspected he would be grateful for it when he stepped outside into the bitter cold morning that awaited him.

"I tried to stop them assigning you to the fishing boat, you know," she said quietly.

He looked up at her, but she wouldn't make eye contact with him. She stared at the floor as she wrung her hands.

"What do you mean?"

"I wanted to have you assigned here to help me, but Mannering is hell bent on taking you out onto the water. For some reason, he thinks you have no respect for him and wants to prove a point. It's a complete turnaround from his stance when you got here. I don't like it."

"I have no issue with him. If he thinks otherwise that's his problem not mine." Ethan said.

"He's a stubborn man. Just be careful out there, that's all."

"It's fishing. How dangerous can it be?" he said, the comment almost making him laugh. They both knew the answer but were unwilling to speak about it.

She didn't offer a response, and so he finished his food in silence. When he was done, he stood. He expected she might at least say something then, but she wouldn't look at him.

"It will be alright, I'll be fine out there," he said.

"No, that's what they all say. All the ones who don't come back," she replied, still staring at the wall.

"I promise, I'll be fine. I'm not afraid of John Mannering."

She looked at him then, her one good eye wet with tears. "It's not John Mannering you need to worry about, and we both know it."

He stood for a few seconds, unsure of the next move, then realising there with nothing else to do or say, he left her alone and headed towards the dock.

TWO

It was a cold, grey morning, and a foggy rain hung in the air. Mannering and Barnes were waiting for him at the dock, loading supplies onto the ninety-foot vessel, the paint on its hull flaking and lined with rust. It bobbed gently against the jetty with the swells of the ocean. At its rear, a huge rusted winch and roll of chain hung out over the ocean. Barnes nodded as he approached. Mannering said nothing, his greeting reduced to a glare. Ethan stared at the boat. The fact that it was the same one from the journal Mannering had given him made it all the more real to him, and for the first time, fear overtook excitement.

"You made it," Barnes said, his breath fogging in the cold air.

"I said I would," Ethan replied.

He looked again at the boat, the fear growing and spreading.

"Don't worry," Barnes said, reading his expression. "You'll be fine. We're not going out too far today. Just a few miles to ease you in. How's the head?"

"It's fine," Ethan muttered. He looked out over the fog-shrouded ocean and felt a chill in his spine which had nothing to do with the temperature.

"You wanna give me a hand with this?" Barnes said, nodding to the crate at his feet. Ethan grabbed the handle at the other end. Any idea of psyching himself up to get on board the boat was gone. Barnes went first, stepping over the edge onto the deck. He followed, unable to help glancing down at the gap between dock and ocean as he stepped across it.

"Thanks, you can just set this down here," Barnes said, lowering his end of the crate.

"Alright, here's how this will work. This is just a two-day trip. We will be heading out now and should be back by tomorrow night. We have supplies in the galley enough to last an extra day or two if we happen to get delayed, but I doubt that will happen. We're heading to a known spot where we should be able to catch something fairly easily. Shallow waters are pretty safe, so I don't want you stressing."

"What's in the box?" Ethan asked, nodding to the crate they just carried on board.

"Bait."

"What kind of bait?" he asked, as the journal he had read sprang back to mind.

"Fish bait. What else?" Barnes asked.

"That box was heavy. That's a lot of bait for a two-day trip."

"Need to catch a lot of fish, what with all the extra mouths we have to feed now," Mannering grunted as he walked past them and into the boat.

"Don't mind him," Barnes said. "He gets a bit intense at times."

"And drunk. I can smell it on him now."

"Yah, well, everyone deals with the world in different ways. He finds peace in the bottle. Don't worry, I'll keep an eye on him. He knows I won't let him go too far."

"I don't know what his problem is with me."

"It's not you. He gets stressed when we go out on these trips. It's a lot of responsibility on his head. A lot of things can go wrong out there. Actually, that reminds me."

"What?"

"Mannering is the only one of us with experience of fishing. He knows what to do. More importantly, he knows how to do it. On land, I run the show. I'm the go-to guy who makes the decisions. Out there, he's the boss, and we do as he says when he says it. Now, I'll give you fair warning. He might give you a little grief, a little hassle. Just ignore it. It's his way of testing you."

"Why would he want to test me? I haven't done anything to him."

"It's just his way, that's all. Try to ignore it. I'll keep him in line. Some kind of fisherman's code. Old school stuff mostly. Give the new guy a hard time to make him earn his stripes."

"Alright, thanks. I appreciate it."

"Don't worry, this will be a straightforward trip." Barnes slapped Ethan on the shoulder then followed Mannering inside the boat, leaving Ethan out alone on deck. He stood at the stern, looking into the murky water. Something inside was nagging at him, that instinct he had so far survived by paying attention to was now telling him that he was about to make a huge mistake.

Mannering appeared at the interior door, the sound of his heavy boots heralding his arrival. "When you've finished standing there doing nothing, you can cast off those lines."

He was gone again before Ethan could respond, disappearing into the vessel.

Ethan looked at the village and its building scattered up the hillside. Although he hadn't been there for long, it was the closest thing to a home he had ever had, and the urge to get off the boat and stay there was strong. He couldn't do it though. He knew it was impossible. He had a job to do. And do it he would. The boat's engines spluttered to life, chimney by the wheelhouse spewing acrid diesel into the air. Ethan untied the lines, stern first, then the bow. He returned to the stern, watching the village shrink away as they moved to open waters. As the village was taken by the heavy fog, Ethan wondered just what he was getting himself into.

#

He never expected to be sick.

Ethan leaned over the side of the boat and vomited into the dull waters. Barnes watched him, not quite able to hide his smile.

"Not exactly the same as the postcard, is it?"

Ethan wiped his mouth and looked at Barnes. "I'll be fine."

"I know you will. Just try not to fall in." Barnes squinted at the sky. "Looks like rain. Come on into the wheelhouse. With the wind the way it is, you'll catch a cold, then you'll really be in for it."

Ethan followed Barnes inside. The wheelhouse was small and cluttered. A narrow staircase led down to the galley kitchen and bunks. At the front of the wheelhouse, Mannering was at the controls and taking them further out to sea. A small table with a bench around three sides of it took up the rest of the space. Barnes slid in first, and Ethan followed. He was glad to be out of the cold and even more relieved that his sickness was starting to fade. He still couldn't shake the weird feeling of actually being in the place where the journal Mannering had given him had taken place. If the intention had been to unsettle him, it had done a fine job.

Ethan could sense Barnes watching him and decided to speak first before he was asked any questions he was uncomfortable answering.

"So where are we heading?

"A little spot that's been kind to us of late around six miles out. It's a nursery of sorts for these creatures we are going hunt. They are a size we can handle with a boat like this."

"How big are they?" Ethan asked, thoughts of the giant behemoth from the journal in his mind.

Barnes considered. "Maybe ten to fifteen feet."

"That's pretty big," Ethan said.

"They grow bigger, especially out in deeper waters. We stick to where it's relatively safe and shallow. Minimum risk for maximum gain."

"How much bigger?" Ethan asked.

Barnes glanced at Mannering again. "I'm not the one to ask about that," he said.

Ethan was about to speak and tell Barnes about the journal, when Mannering spoke. He didn't look towards them, he kept his eyes firmly on the landscape of waves in front of the boat.

"Five years ago, I saw one. A big one. It's passed where we're going now, out where it's deep and dark." He stopped the boat, killing the engines and bringing a curtain of silence down on the wheelhouse. The vessel rocked from side to side, carried by the tides. Mannering finally turned to face them, looking at them in turn, rocking with the boat as it was pushed by the choppy ocean. "We got lost and ended up badly off course. Found ourselves fifty miles out to sea. We'd stopped to plot a course back to the village when we saw it off the starboard bow coming towards us just under the surface."

"What are they?"

Mannering shrugged. "You read that book I gave you. You know the story. Those things are nothing that wasn't there before. It's just changed into something else. Merged together by the event. Two creatures or more melted together into something new."

"You showed him the book?" Barnes said, glaring at Mannering. "Jesus, John, I told you not to do that. It's too soon."

"I thought he needed to know if you were insisting on bringing him out here."

"It's alright, it's done now," Ethan said, wanting to avoid adding any more tension to the atmosphere.

Mannering looked at them both and continued his story. "Anyway, we saw this thing coming towards the boat. It was a big one. Forty feet at least. I reckon they don't probably get much bigger than that, even though that little red book I gave you claims on a two-hundred footer, I doubt it's true and thank God for that. Even at fifteen feet, these things are lethal. Fishermen like to exaggerate sizes of their catch." Mannering grimaced. "The thing you have to understand about these creatures is that all of us are out here for the same thing. We come out to hunt them, and they, in turn, hunt us. They know that when our boats are out here, they have food on them. That makes things interesting and dangerous." He reached over the console and grabbed a clear bottle of brownish liquid with a cork stopper. He opened it and took a drink, the pungent smell of homebrew whisky filling the room.

"Something that big could easily destroy a boat of this size," Ethan said

Mannering nodded. "Now you're starting to get it. See, we don't come out here and hope they don't see us. We bait them. We tell them we're here, like ringing the dinner bell. They come to eat, then it's a case of who kills who first."

"That's why we stick to the area where we're heading, with the juveniles." Barnes cut in, glaring at Mannering as he took another drink.

Ethan took a moment to let it all sink in. "This is dangerous."

He wasn't saying it to let Barnes or Mannering know. They were already more than aware. He said it in order to confirm it to himself.

"Now he gets it," Mannering said. "Now he understands that it's not all about picture postcards and the love of the sea. This is life and death, make no mistake about it. You want to know why I didn't want you out here, there you have it."

"Another thing," Barnes said as Mannering returned to the controls of the boat and started the engine. "They are incredibly aggressive. Incredibly dangerous. Even the ones we're heading out to take now could kill us with ease. They're clever bastards too. This is a first for you, and you need to go easy. We've lost a lot of good men out on these waters because they got over confident."

"We don't need to get into that right now. Ethan doesn't need to hear about that," Barnes replied.

"I think he does," Mannering cut in. "I think he needs to hear in great detail about how each and every one of them were lost."

"Yeah, well I think you've had enough to drink for now, John. This isn't the time."

Mannering glared at him then put the bottle back. The three of them were silent, doing all they could to avoid conversation.

"We're almost there," Mannering said as he changed direction slightly. "You both better get used to why we're out here and get your head straight. It's almost game time."

Barnes slid out from the table and headed for the rear deck. "Come on and help me with the bait."

Ethan followed, struggling to control his nerves

Barnes stood by the large box they had brought on board. "Grab that other end," he said as he crouched by it. Ethan looked out over the dirty ocean, then did as he was told. Together, they pried the lid off the box. Ethan wretched at the smell. Inside was a bloated, bloody carcass of some kind of animal.

"What is it?" Ethan asked, covering his mouth.

"Pig. We fattened it up as much as we could before bringing it out here. It should draw one of those things straight to us."

Barnes words about fattening up the pig brought back memories of the cage McCarthy had kept him in, and he shuddered.

"You alright?" Barnes asked.

"Yeah, I'm fine."

"Alright, then let's do this."

They tipped the box onto its side, spilling the bloody carcass onto the deck. Barnes grabbed the reel of chain at the rear of the boat. At the end of it, were two barbed hooks, their points sharpened.

"Alright, let's hook this thing on and get it over the side."

Together, they embedded the hooks into the belly of the creature, then wrapped the chain around it to hold it in position as the boat came to a stop.

Mannering appeared at the deck door, watching them. "Make sure you wrap that good and tight," he said.

Ethan glanced at him then continued to help secure the carcass.

"Alright I think we're good," Barnes said. He walked over to the winch controls. "Stand back and we can get this stinking thing overboard."

Barnes activated the controls for the winch, reeling in the chain and lifting the carcass into the air. "Alright, shove it out over the rear of the boat."

Ethan complied, shoving the carcass hard and watching as the winch boom swung with its prize over the ocean. As Ethan watched, the winch began to lower the pig into the water. He let out around five feet of chain, then stopped.

"That's still close to the boat," Ethan said.

"Has to be," Mannering said as he joined them. He was holding two harpoon guns. "We need him in close so we can tag him."

"What if it hits us?"

Mannering grinned. "I think you're finally starting to see that this isn't all fun and games out here."

"I never said it was."

"You'll learn yet. Here, grab this." Mannering tossed him the harpoon gun. It was heavier than it looked, and he almost dropped it.

"Careful with that," Mannering said, flashing another wild grin. "I don't want to send you over for it if you drop it in the water."

Ethan ignored the comment. He looked at the bloated pig bobbing just below the surface, then at Barnes. "What now?"

"Now, we wait until one of them comes to take the bait."

"How will we know?"

"Trust me, you'll know. As soon as it takes the bait, you take your shot. The harpoon is on a cable. We have around three hundred feet of line so we should be good. That cable is strong, thick. The dart is designed to open up on entry. The idea is you hit him in the soft part of its belly so the barbs hold it in place. After that, we hook the wire onto the winch here. Hopefully, he'll have swallowed the bait and hook too by then, meaning we have a good grip on him."

"Then what?" Ethan asked, thinking the plan felt more and more reckless as it was told.

Mannering grinned. "Then we nail gun him. Boom. Through the brain. Big nails, five inchers. They go right into his head and kill him without a fight."

"That's the theory," Barnes said, giving a wayward glance to Mannering.

"What do you mean?" Ethan asked.

"He means sometimes the nail gun don't work, or if it does, it only goes part way in. That makes our big fish mad. That's when people start getting themselves killed."

"Go easy on him, the kid doesn't need to hear that right now," Barnes said, glaring at the older man.

"Maybe I disagree."

"Drop it, John. Not now. Not here."

Mannering looked at Barnes, desperate to respond. In the end, he snorted and glared at Ethan. "You never should have come out here, kid."

He walked away, disappearing back into the belly of the boat.

"Thanks," Ethan said as he watched Mannering leave.

"Don't listen to him. He always gets uptight when we come out here."

"How long has he been with you?"

Barnes shrugged. "A long time. He was one of the first in our group."

"He seems a little…off. Likes his drink too, I've noticed."

"Yeah, well, the world does that to a lot of people, especially how it is now. It's not a good place. The drinking is a problem, but I'm managing it, or at least I'm trying to. Back home, he drinks until he passes out. Here, I keep a tight leash on him."

"Is it safe to be around him?" Ethan asked, wondering if he was the only one who could see how unhinged Mannering was.

"He's right enough. A few screws loose, but he's a damn good fisherman and has made sure we keep food on our tables for the last few years."

"I don't like him. He's…" Ethan let it hang, unable to find the right word.

"Unstable," Barnes said, finding it for him. "True enough, maybe he is. In the old world, he'd have been shunned and incarcerated. Hell, even in this one with all the bad people out there, the same could have happened. I'm not about to do that though, not when it's my show to run, and the people of this town are looking to me to lead them. God only knows there has been enough bloodshed and pain. Now is about rebuilding."

"To like it was before?"

Barnes shook his head. "It will never be like it was before. That world, that way of living, is gone. Finished. What we can do is try to learn from the mistakes those before us made and make it better. Seems to me Mother Nature wiped the slate clean and left a few of us behind to start again."

"Is that even possible?"

"Not in my lifetime, or yours most likely. But a generation or two from now, maybe they'll have crops and fresh food, and won't have to resort to coming out here and doing crazy stuff like this."

Ethan looked out at the ocean. He could no longer see land. "So what do we do now?"

"We wait."

"How long?"

"Until our fish is hungry."

THREE

It was hard to gauge how much time had passed. The initial excitement and fear about the creature they were about to encounter had dulled into a restless boredom. Mannering had gone back to the wheelhouse. Barnes was sitting with his back to the stern, eyes closed, legs out in front of him. Ethan perched on the transom. He watched the water ebb and flow as it gently rocked the boat. Ethan could feel his eyes growing heavy as he looked at the water. He tried to imagine it as it once was. Blue and clean instead of dull and brown. It was then that something caught his eye. He stood, focussing on the water, making sure it wasn't his eyes playing tricks on him.

"Barnes," he said, his voice a whisper lodged in his throat. "Barnes," he said again, making himself heard.

Barnes got up and stood beside him, looking out to the rear of the boat. "Looks like someone is interested in our bait," he said.

The two watched as the wake rolled closer to the boat, angling towards the putrid corpse which hung a few feet below the waterline at the rear of the boat.

"Steady now," Barnes said, his voice a near whisper. "Let her have a look at what we're offering."

The wake skimmed past the boat, cautiously passing the offered food. Ethan leaned over the edge of the transom, watching as it passed. It was around sixteen feet long, its body a mottled grey-brown. It looked exactly like Mannering had said. It was unlike any one creature. Instead, it was a twisted combination of things. The main bulk of the body looked as if it had once been a whale, but it sprouted thick milky-coloured tentacles from its underside. On the top of its head, a bulbous lump which looked like another head, complete with array of black eyes and a half-formed, razor-toothed mouth melded into the body of the main creature. It propelled itself on its deformed fins, its fluke tapering to a point attached to which was a large, misshaped flipper.

"Fifteen foot, I reckon," Mannering said, startling Ethan who hadn't heard him join them at the stern.

"Let's hope it takes the bait then we can snag it and get out of here."

The creature returned, swimming close to the offered bait, nudging it with a flipper then moving away.

"What is it doing? Ethan asked, the words catching in his throat.

"They do that sometimes," Mannering said, answering the question directed at Barnes. "They're cautious of us now, they know what we're out here for."

"We should get the harpoon ready," Barnes said, turning towards it.

"Let the new kid do it."

Barnes looked at Mannering. "He's not ready for that yet. This is his first time out here."

"He wants to earn his place, doesn't he?"

"That's not the point, and you know it."

"Why not? We all had to do it. All of us had to do this for the first time once. Why not him now?"

"This isn't a game."

"I ain't laughing," Mannering said

"It's alright," Ethan said, interjecting before an argument could break out. "I'll do it if you show me how."

Barnes glared at Mannering, who was sneering at him, then turned his attention to Ethan. "You don't have to do it. Don't let him get to you."

"He's right though," Ethan replied. "I was the one who wanted to come out here. I should earn my keep."

"You don't have to. Nobody will think any less of you."

Ethan was desperate to take the get-out offered by Mannering. He wanted no part of those awful things which existed in the ocean. It dawned on him then that the place he had always seen as the one thing of beauty in his life was in reality just as horrific as the rest of the world. He wasn't sure he would ever go back on the ocean again.

He was about to say all this to Barnes when Mannering spoke again. "Careful, boy. Is that your pussy I can hear clenching up there?"

Ethan turned to Mannering, then back to Barnes. "No, it's alright. I want to do this."

It was clear Barnes was angry, but he knew Mannering was volatile and tipsy, and not someone he should aggravate. He instead picked up the harpoon and handed it to Ethan.

"Alright, get used to the weight of it. Now when you fire, this thing will kick upwards. To compensate, you need to aim a little lower than you would normally."

Ethan nodded, trying to hide how scared he was.

"Have you ever fired a weapon of this size before?"

Ethan shook his head.

"Come on, she's gonna take the bait. Get on with it," Mannering barked as he watched the creature make another cautious approach at the bait.

Barnes ignored him. "Try and get him side on, under or near the flipper. Don't worry about it too much, but somewhere in that general area will do it."

"What if I miss?"

Barnes grinned, but it was forced. "Try not to. It's not the end of the world if you do, but we'd rather not lose any gear."

"Come on, what are you both waiting for?" Mannering snapped.

"In a minute," Barnes replied.

"In a minute? You think this thing will wait?"

Barnes ignored him and looked Ethan in the eye. "You can do this. Just relax, got it?"

Ethan nodded and swung the harpoon out over the stern of the boat. It was heavy, and his arms were already burning. He could feel Mannering's gaze on him just waiting for him to make a mistake. He concentrated on the water, waiting for the creature to break the surface. Although he couldn't see it, he could sense it there, out in the deep.

For a moment, there was quiet. The steady lap of waves on the hull, the creak of tired wood as the boat drifted with the tide. Even Mannering was silent, all three of them watching the water.

"There it is," Mannering said. He pointed, but there was little need. They could all see it. The wake was coming towards the rear of the boat, this time there was no indecision. It was heading straight for the carcass.

"You be ready now. Don't you miss the son of a bitch," Mannering muttered.

Ethan heard him, but he was distant. Nothing outside of the wake existed. He watched it, frozen and unable to move. He was aware of everything going on around him in minute detail. The warmth of the diffused sun on his neck, the unsteady sway of the boat, the slightly musty, boozy sweat smell of Mannering who was now standing close. He closed one eye, focussing on his aim.

"Not yet," Mannering said from somewhere close by.

Ethan forced himself to relax and let out the breath he had been unknowingly holding. The absolute idiocy of the situation almost made him giggle, but he knew that wouldn't be the right thing to do, so swallowed it down.

"Wait until it takes the bait and tries to run with it. When you get a clear shot, take your shot. Remember to aim low," Barnes said, his own voice also a near whisper.

The creature breached the surface, a disfigured, mottled abomination from hell. Ethan couldn't imagine how such a thing could have survived. It opened its mouth and clamped down on the putrid carcass, the boat dipping towards the creature tugging on the winch cable. Ethan moved his finger over the trigger.

"Wait, damn you," Mannering hissed.

The creature had clamped on to the carcass and had now flicked out a disfigured tentacle, which it coiled around its meal. It started to thrash and pull, the stern of the vessel dipping closer to the water.

"We need to let out a little of that winch line," Barnes said. Although Mannering was standing by the release handle, he didn't move. His eyes were alternating between Ethan and the creature. Barnes skirted around Ethan and released the tension on the cable, glaring at Mannering.

"Don't let too much of that out, you hear?" the old fisherman said.

Barnes clamped the release valve closed, slamming it into place. He ignored Mannering and returned to his original position, both men now at either side of Ethan. With the cable slack, the creature was able to thrash and pull at the carcass without putting the boat in danger.

"Get ready. Don't miss this," Mannering said, leaning on the transom, his muscular forearms rippling. Of all of them, he seemed to be least afraid. If anything, he seemed to be enjoying the show.

"Now, do it now," Barnes said.

Ethan refocused on the creature. It had half turned as it rolled with the bait, tangling itself in the winch cable at the same time. Ethan aimed for the spot he wanted, the fleshy area above the flipper, then moved his aim down a half foot and depressed the trigger.

Mannering was right about the kick. The barrel of the harpoon jerked up as he fired, the barbed harpoon hitting home almost exactly where he had intended. The creature lurched and thrashed, covering the three men with spray as it wrapped itself tighter in the winch cable.

"Let out some more cable," Barnes said as the creature rolled closer to the boat, again causing the stern to dip dangerously close to the water level.

Mannering grabbed the release lever and pulled it, expecting the hiss of the winch releasing and feeding out more line; however, there was no change. The handle didn't move. For the first time, Mannering looked afraid.

"Damn things jammed," he grunted. He grabbed it with both hands, desperately trying to release the tension. Ethan was still holding the harpoon, unable to take his eyes off the power of the creature as it thrashed against its restraints and threatened to sink them too.

Barnes ran to help, the two men yanking at the handle to try and free the mechanism. Ethan was too terrified to move. The creature had rolled itself into the winch cable in a way that would be impossible to free itself from. Now that it was so close to the rear of the boat, its size and power could be fully appreciated. It could easily destroy the vessel. The realisation that they could all die kicked Ethan into action. He dropped the harpoon and climbed onto the transom of the boat, his feet just inches from the churning ocean and the thrashing creature beyond. He could see where the cable had slipped off the spool and become tangled. He pulled at it, desperately trying to free it, but it was too tight with the creature hanging off the end of it. The steel frame of the winch was starting to groan under the pressure, and the filthy floorboards were starting to splinter.

"We'll get pulled under if we don't free the cable," Mannering grunted.

Barnes looked over his shoulder and saw Ethan standing on the transom. "Down, get down from there," he screamed and left

Mannering with the release lever.

"It's come off the spool," Ethan replied.

"Get down, let me take a look."

Ethan turned to comply, when the creature lurched, pulling the boat dangerously low in the water. He reached out for the frame of the winch, but couldn't stop himself from slipping. His heart lurched into his throat as he went overboard hitting the water just a few feet from the thrashing creature. He didn't know how to swim and took an involuntary deep breath, taking on water and starting to choke as he thrashed around.

I'm going to die.

He was surprised how calm the thought came to him. He supposed it was a side effect of the world he lived in. He was about to give up all hope, when he was pulled out of the water by Barnes.

"Grab on," he bellowed as Ethan gripped the inner edge of the transom and pulled himself up and over, falling onto the deck, too afraid to do anything but watch. He saw it all in slow motion framed against the dull grey sky. Mannering trying to free the winch handle, Barnes leaning over the edge, hacking away at the cable itself, teeth gritted as the boat shrieked and groaned as it was pulled closer and closer to the edge of the water, and with it, death. Then, something else. Something blotting the day from view, something huge and greenish, a spinal ridge covered in scars and barnacles moving across his field of view. In the back of his mind, he knew what it was, but he couldn't comprehend it. The sheer size, the sheer scale. It was at least five times larger than the one currently attached to the winch. It breached the water, mouth opening, teeth glistening and needle sharp as it closed on the rear of the struggling creature. It severed it in two, blood and water exploding and showering those on the boat, which lurched up, the winch freed from the decimated half of the creature that remained as the giant took its meal back into the darkness of the ocean. For a brief second, there was absolute silence, then there was screaming. Barnes was staggering around the deck, his arm cleanly severed when the larger creature attacked. Blood in impossible quantities covered the deck, a river of it. All Ethan could see were the whites of Barnes's eyes.

"Help me with him," Mannering said, shouting above the screams.

Ethan couldn't move, he replayed it in his mind, the size if the creature. He knew now why Mannering was so against his love of the sea. He knew what was out there, and now Ethan did too.

"Fucking get up and help me," Mannering screamed again.

Ethan scrambled to his feet, shivering from a combination of cold and shock. "What do I do?"

"Take your belt off, tighten it around the arm above the wound," Mannering shouted. He guided Barnes towards the interior of the boat, the deck now covered in spilled blood.

"That thing, did you see it? It was huge, we need to get out of here." Ethan knew he was rambling, but knew of no other way to handle what was happening.

"You take off that belt and make him a tourniquet, or I swear to God, I'll dump you over the side," Mannering growled, glaring at Ethan.

Ethan nodded and took off his frayed canvas belt.

"Good, now tie it round the top of the arm. Make sure it's tight."

Barnes' skin had taken on a colour similar to that of the overcast sky, and he had stopped screaming. Ethan did as Mannering said, tying the belt around the wound and just above the elbow.

"Make sure it's tight," Mannering grunted as they led him towards the small dining table. Mannering swept the plates and dishes off it, and together, the two of them put Barnes on the table, the blood still freely pouring from him. Ethan finished tying the belt and pulled it tight. Barnes screamed and tried to sit up, but together Mannering and Ethan kept him in place.

"We need to get him back and get some help," Ethan said, double typing the makeshift tourniquet.

Mannering pointed to a cupboard across the room. "Towels are in there, see what you can do to keep him alive."

"Are we heading in?"

"Yeah, you stay here with him," Mannering grunted as he went to the controls and fired up the engines.

Ethan found the towels; they were grubby, but that was something he couldn't afford to worry about right now. He went back to Barnes and put some under the wound, the blood immediately soaking through. The others he tried to use to dress the injury. Barnes was pale, his eyes heavy as he lay on the table.

"It's alright, we're heading in," Ethan said, watching as one by one the towels turned red.

Barnes looked at him. "Did you see it? Did you…?"

"I saw it," Ethan said quietly.

"I've never seen one that big. Nobody has…" Barnes muttered. He stared at Ethan as the boat rocked and lurched over the waves. "I'm going to die out here."

"You won't, we'll get you back in time," Ethan said, wishing he could sound more positive and assured.

"He won't be heading back," Barnes mumbled.

"He is, we're going back."

Barnes shook his head. "He'll be going after it. I know him."

Ethan glanced at Mannering's back. It was impossible to tell which direction they were going through the grimy windows. He turned back to Barnes, who was staring at him. Ethan stood and walked to the controls, standing behind Mannering and looking for the first smudge of shore.

"How far out are we? He's in bad shape."

"Mind your business. I'll mind mine," Mannering said, without taking his eyes off the ocean.

"He needs help."

"Then go look after him. Make yourself useful."

"Mannering, I –"

Ahead of them, the water broke and a marbled, arched back appeared, a plume of spray ejected from the giant creatures blowhole before it descended again beneath the surface.

"What are you doing?" Ethan said, staring at Mannering.

"I told you to mind your business."

"I am minding my business. We need to get back, not give chase to this…thing. It's too big. We can't handle it."

Mannering turned and glared at him. Ethan could see he was scared, even though it was projecting itself as anger. "And what do you know? You've been here five minutes trying to tell me my business. I've been doing this a long time, way before you showed up."

"Barnes needs our help."

"And those people back at the village don't?" Mannering snapped. "What are they supposed to eat when we come back empty handed?"

"Mannering, think about this. You saw how big that thing was. We can't possibly catch it. It would crush us. Barnes needs medical attention."

"Did you apply the tourniquet?"

"Yes."

"And use the towels to bandage the injury?"

"Yes."

"Then there's nothing else we can do. He wouldn't want us to go back."

"You're crazy, this is crazy."

Mannering glanced at him and grinned. "You read that book I gave you, you know how it is out here."

"And you know how it ended. Mannering, please…"

Mannering moved quickly. He turned and grabbed Ethan around the throat, pushing him back against the wall, their faces inches apart. "I told you that you didn't belong out here. I tried to tell Barnes you had no business out here but he didn't listen. Now he's hurt and that's on him. I'm a fisherman, goddamnit, and I'm going to fish."

Mannering let go of Ethan and turned back to the controls of the boat. "Now you do whatever you have to in order to keep him alive, but we're going after this fish. You know how much food there is on it? How long it will keep us going?"

"With one less mouth to feed when Barnes is dead."

"That's on you," Mannering said.

"No, it's on you, and I'll make sure to tell them all you did this."

Mannering glanced over his shoulder, the wild look still there in his eyes. "You think they'll believe you? A stranger they are already wary of? A man who, if we look at it like it is, was responsible for what happened to Barnes?"

"How was it my fault?"

"You had no business being out here; you fell in the water, and he had to save you. If that hadn't happened, then his arm wouldn't have been in the way, and that thing wouldn't have got him."

"And what about you? When they find out you ignored his injuries and came out here chasing after that thing."

Mannering spun around and pointed at Ethan. "They will understand when I drag that big son of a bitch in. When they know our future is secure, when they know I've just put food on the table enough for everyone, they'll understand well enough."

"That won't happen," Ethan said, walking back towards Barnes.

"Why not?"

"Because we'll die before then. If you try to take that thing on, you'll lose."

CHAPTER SEVEN

For the next twelve hours, Mannering gave chase to the creature, taking them further and further away from safety. Ethan stayed with Barnes, tending to his injuries as best he could, but the water bottles they had brought with them were almost empty and the towels were all soaked through with blood. Ethan listened to Barnes mumble as he drifted in and out of consciousness, taking to people who weren't there and reliving old memories from a different lifetime. Death was close, and both Ethan and Barnes could feel it. Mannering was oblivious, and saw nothing but the creature as it came up for air, ensuring he stayed close enough not to lose sight of it. Ethan had checked the supplies and there was precious little. He sat by Barnes and put his head in his hands.

"You have to stop him."

Ethan looked at Barnes, who was staring at him.

"How can I stop him?"

"You have to. We'll die out here otherwise. We don't have enough supplies to survive. If you don't stop him, we're all dead."

"He's stronger than me, I can't do it."

Barnes tried to speak, then started to cough, fresh blood spilling down his chin. "There's a baseball bat in the galley," he grunted. "Use that. He'll back down if you threaten him."

Ethan was afraid, his eyes shifted to the steps leading down the galley, then at Mannering, who was still preoccupied with his pursuit. The light was fading from the sky, and the idea of being out there at night with such a giant in the ocean terrified him more than Mannering.

"Alright," he said, "I'll do it."

"Go now, do it now. I don't know how much longer I can hold on."

The thought of being alone with Mannering on the boat if Barnes died spurred him into action. He stood, Mannering glancing over his shoulder.

"Going somewhere?" Mannering said.

"We need more towels for the bleeding. I'm going to see if there's anything below."

"Some sheets in the bunks maybe," Mannering said as he turned back to the controls. "Try there."

Ethan said nothing, surprised at how relaxed Mannering seemed under the circumstances. Ethan went below deck and found what he was looking for, the bat pitted with age and dirt. He held it in his right hand, hoping it would make him feel strong and confident, but instead it was fear he felt. It battled him, trying to sway him from what he knew he had to do in order to survive. Mannering wasn't thinking rationally, that much was obvious, but Ethan still didn't know if they would understand when he got back why he had taken over the boat, especially if Barnes didn't make it. If that happened, it would be Mannering's word against his, a stranger who was new to their group and hadn't earned their respect or trust.

He pushed those thoughts aside. He couldn't let them influence his decision. Barnes was right. He had to act now before it was too late. He went back to the upper deck, his heart thumping, the engines humming as Mannering drove them further and further out to sea. He was sure his approach was masked by the sounds of the engine, but even so, every creak of tired floorboard felt incredibly loud to him. He crept forward, glancing towards Barnes, who had lifted his head up to watch. Mannering was still staring out to sea, watching for the creature breaching. Ethan stopped six feet away.

"Mannering, stop the boat."

He paid no attention.

"I said stop the boat."

Mannering glanced over his shoulder, saw the bat, and then turned back to the controls. "If you're planning on using that, boy, you better make sure you do it right."

"I'll do it if I have to. Stop the boat."

"You won't do it. People like you aren't cut out for this world."

"I'll do it. Stop the boat."

"Not now, boy. We're close to him now. He's getting tired. All that meat, all that sweet meat to feed everyone."

Ethan took another step closer, holding the bat ready to swing. "Stop the boat."

Mannering sighed and shook his head. "You don't understand, do you, boy? You're not a survivor. You are alive by some kind of miracle. People like you, the weak, most of them died off years ago, yet somehow you survived. Somehow you lived long enough to get here, to this point. The odds of that are pretty high, don't you think?"

It was clear that Mannering was unafraid, which in turn was terrifying Ethan.

"I'm in control here," Ethan said, but it sounded weak and he knew it.

"I can't blame you, I suppose," Mannering went on, adjusting his course slightly. "You kids don't remember what it was like before, when there was still hope, still something to look forward to in this world. Now it's just sand and death. Your generation are lucky. You don't know how it was so you don't miss it."

He glanced over his shoulder again, ignoring the bat and looking Ethan in the eye. "I remember. I miss it, and I know this world we live in now is hell, so if you're going to hit me with that thing then do it, but know this. I'm not afraid, not like you. If you come at me, do it right, because you can bet I'll come right back at you. Only difference is, I won't hesitate. I won't fail."

"Please, I'm asking you to stop. I know we got off on the wrong foot, but we can fix this. We need to get Barnes back to town."

"And do what? Save him? Get him to a doctor? Let me tell you something, kid. There are no doctors, not anymore. There isn't anyone who can help. All it means is there is one less mouth to feed. It's just a matter of time before he dies and you and I both know it."

"We have to try."

"No."

Ethan adjusted his grip on the bat. "Then you don't leave me any choice."

He took a step forward, readying his swing, but Mannering spun to meet him, firing the flare gun at Ethan. It hit him in the shoulder, knocking him off his feet and sending the bat rolling across the floor.

The agony was unreal, the burning in his shoulder radiating through his entire body. He couldn't move his arm, or catch his breath, all he could was lie there and wait to die. Mannering appeared in his field of vision, standing above him. Ethan saw that he was now holding the baseball bat which he held casually, the business end resting on his shoulder.

"That was stupid, kid. Now I think you finally understand."

There was so much Ethan wanted to say, but he couldn't. He could barely breathe. He wanted to beg and plead, but it was too late. He watched as Mannering swung the bat at his prone head, then his entire world became dark.

CHAPTER EIGHT

Ethan woke, the pain in his head radiating through his entire body. He opened his eyes and peered into the gloom. He was in the galley kitchen, his hands tied around a pipe on the wall. His shoulder screamed in agony, but the throbbing in his head was worse. He could barely open one of his eyes.

"You're awake."

He hadn't seen Mannering sitting in the corner. He was just a shape amid the shadows. Apart from the creaking of the boat as it rocked with the tides, there was absolute silence.

"You didn't kill me," Ethan mumbled, his words slurring.

"No, I didn't."

Ethan didn't like not being able to see Mannering's face or read his expression.

"Why have you tied me up?"

"For my own safety, you were going to attack me."

"I just wanted you to stop." As he said it, Ethan remembered the reasons why he wanted to go back in the first place. "Barnes, how is Barnes?"

Mannering didn't reply. He sat for a moment, then answered. "We are out of fuel. Did you know that?"

"How are we going to get back? We need help."

"Plus food. And water."

"I told you this would happen. I told you we had to go back."

"You did," Mannering said, his voice soft and without anger. "That you did. It seems on this occasion, the coward's way was the correct one."

"So what do we do now?"

"It's already done," Mannering said. "It was necessary."

He flicked on the light. What was left of Barnes was in a plastic tub by the door, his remaining arm and both legs severed, his torso wedged in behind them. Barnes dead eyes stared, and his mouth was open. Ethan tried to squirm away from it, but his restraints were tight.

"What did you do? What the hell did you do to him?"

"I put him out of his misery," Mannering said, resting a hand on the bloody, matted hair of Barnes's corpse. "He was dying anyway, he'd lost too much blood. He'd want it this way though. He'd want us to do whatever it took to survive."

"You're insane, you killed him. You murdered him over a...a fish."

Mannering crossed the room and crouched in front of Ethan, his eyes wild and alive with madness. "We've all done things we ain't proud of. Me included. But we have us a little situation here and I need you, boy. I need you to step up and prove yourself."

Ethan was afraid. He tried to look Mannering in the eye, but couldn't do it. Instead, he stared at his hands, his wrists raw from struggling against the rope.

"Like I said, boy. We're out of fuel and drifting. We got no food. No water. I had to take a decision. Barnes as already gone the second that bastard took his arm. Even if we'd have got him back, the infection would have finished him."

Ethan glanced at Mannering, then at the box containing what was left of Barnes behind him. Mannering followed his gaze and stood, walking back towards the door.

"In situations like this, there isn't an option. Barnes is a dead man, and we will need food. Meat."

"Meat? You mean..." Ethan shook his head.

"It's food, ain't it?" Mannering snapped. "We also need bait."

"Bait? Are you insane? We're out of fuel, we have nothing.

You can't go out there still trying to chase that monster."

"That's what I'm saying to you, boy. I know that. God knows I know it now. Only, things have changed. I ain't chasing him anymore. He's hunting us."

"You're lying, just saying things to make what you did right," Ethan said.

"No, I wish I was. See, when you were under, I got real close to him. Jabbed him with the harpoon gun a couple of times, even fired off the other round of the flare gun right into his back. He didn't like that. You know, boy, I always thought these fish were dumb. I don't know why, I just figured that they were that way because they were fish. Not this guy though. He's smart. He knew what would happen, see. He kept running out from the boat, then slowing down, teasing me in, letting me get close, then moving out again. Making me chase, making me go where I didn't want to go. Out where it was deep and far away from home." Mannering grinned and shook his head. "When the fuel ran out, I was partly relieved. You ever hear of the term 'thrill of the chase'?"

Ethan shook his head.

"I supposed as much. It was something from the old world, usually related to when a man would try to get a woman interested enough in him to put out. The chase was the motivator, see, but once the chase was over, often times the man would realise he didn't even really like the woman too much. He just wanted her because she was unavailable. Anyway, that's what happened here. I wanted to catch that big son of a bitch. I wanted it more than I've ever wanted anything in my life, even though I had no idea what I would do if I ever caught it."

Ethan was watching him now, captivated by his story.

"Anyway, around two in the morning, we ran out of fuel. I don't even know if I knew we were that low. Part of me thinks no, I wouldn't have been so stupid, but another part of me thinks maybe I did. Maybe that was going to be my way of justifying to myself why I stopped chasing it. Anyway, the fuel runs out and the boat slows. I'm just sitting there, drifting on the tide, watching for that big bastard to break the surface somewhere in the distance as it went on its way. "

"What happened?"

"It breached, only not where I was expecting it to. Bastard came up right next to the boat. I looked at it, right there, not twenty feet away from me, that big eye of his staring at me, and me back at him, he went under, and I thought he was done until he breached again, this time ahead of the boat, maybe twenty-five feet away. It wanted me to know it was there, see? It was all part of the game."

Mannering stood and walked back across the kitchen. He took a carving knife from the sink which was still streaked with Barnes' blood, then turned back to Ethan. "Do you understand what I'm saying to you?"

Ethan nodded, unsure if he did or not.

Mannering walked slowly back towards him, and pointed the knife at him. "If I cut you lose, you need to tell me you won't do anything dumb. Whatever you might think of me, I ain't a killer. Fair enough, I was riding you pretty hard all the time we were out here, but this is different. Now it's just us. Us and that thing."

"We can't hunt it, it's impossible," Ethan said, unable to take his eyes from the knife blade.

"This isn't about hunting. This is about surviving. You see Barnes over there in that box?"

Ethan nodded. He had no intention of looking again at it.

"Then you know what I'm capable of. I don't want to hurt you or anyone else, but I need you to help me think of a plan. Can I trust you?"

"It works both ways," Ethan replied. "Can I trust you not to come at me or attack me?"

Mannering crouched and held the knife up so Ethan could see it. "I took no pleasure in doing what I did. None at all. That's not me. I'm not a killer like those crazies who walk what's left of this world and kills people for food. I'm a good man."

Mannering cut the ropes tying Ethan to the pipe then stood. "Come with me. You need to see it for yourself," he said, then walked away, heading to the upper deck.

Ethan stood and rubbed his wrists, then glanced at the remains of Barnes, which served as a reminder of just how dangerous a man he was in close proximity with. He followed Mannering upstairs, climbing the narrow staircase to the upper deck.

A hazy dawn as close to breaking, or at least, as close to a dawn as existed in the new world. A murky gloom hung on the ocean, which was gently taking the boat where it pleased on the tides. Mannering was standing out on the rear deck, breath fogging in the cold air. Ethan walked out and stood beside him. Ethan looked at him, then out to sea.

"Where is it?" he asked.

"Right there," Mannering said, nodding to the open expanse of ocean. Ethan looked, the boat creaking and rocking in the silence.

"Where?"

"Somewhere," Mannering replied. "Can't you feel him watching us?"

Ethan glanced at Mannering, his face twisted in concentration as he stared at the ocean. "I don't feel a thing."

"You will. If not now, soon."

"Why soon?" Ethan asked.

"Because he's getting ready to make his move on us, and when he does, we'll kill him."

"How?"

Mannering turned to Ethan and grinned. "That's the fun part. Trying to figure it out."

"Nothing about this is fun. We're going to die out here unless we figure out a way to stop it."

"That we are. Maybe Barnes ain't got it so bad after all."

Ethan was about to reply when the ocean exploded ten feet from them, a jet of freezing water erupting into the air.

"There she is," Mannering whispered. "I told you she was watching."

Ethan stared at it, the creature's eye the size of a basketball as it watched them.

"She never goes too far from her food," Mannering whispered, a small smile on his lips. The creature sank beneath the surface, leaving the ocean flat and calm again.

Ethan turned to Mannering, his guts full of lead. "What do we do, Mannering? You're the expert. You've been out here."

"That I have, but I'm no expert. Not with fish as big as this."

"But you must have an idea, you must have a plan."

"I got a plan," Mannering said. "I'm going to go get myself a little drink of whisky and hope our big fish swims away to bother someone else."

"That's it?" Ethan said as Mannering went back inside. "That's your plan?"

"Unless you have a better one."

Mannering went inside, grabbed the bottle of whisky from one of the cupboards then sat at the table, which was still smeared with dry blood from Barnes. Mannering opened the bottle and took a drink.

"Getting drunk won't help. We have a crisis on our hands here," Ethan said, following Mannering inside.

"You think this is a snap decision? You don't think I've been sat here trying to think of a way when you were knocked out downstairs?" Mannering snapped.

"No, but…"

"No but nothing. I've been over every inch of this boat, and I can't think of anything to do. Now it's your turn. While you do that, I'm going to sit here and drink. Got it?"

"You brought us all the way out here, you can't just sit there and hope this thing goes away, we have to do something to help ourselves."

"Like I said, I'm all ears."

"Mannering…"

"You talk too much, boy. Barnes talked too much, always preaching and sure he knew best, that he knew better than me. People who talk too much often times find themselves in trouble. Big trouble."

The threat was barely veiled, and Ethan received the message loud and clear. He left Mannering to find solace in his bottle and set about trying to figure out what they could use to help them. For two hours, he searched the boat. Checking every cupboard, every place where something useful might be lurking and able to help them, but, much like the world in which they existed, the vessel was barren and devoid of anything but its most basic structure. On a whim, he went into the engine room, hoping that even though they were adrift, there may be something to help. He ducked under and twisted through the snaking network of pipes around the engines, finding nothing but a few oily rags, bolts and loose screws. It was as he was about to give up, that he noticed the fuel gauges on the control panel by the wall. He stared at it, unable to believe what he was seeing. The answer to the problem had been in front of him all along and he hated himself for not seeing it sooner. Mannering was mad, he knew that. Mad and a murderer. Ethan's fault had been that he hadn't realised just how far gone he was. Far enough to murder, that was for sure, but also apparently far enough to commit a long, slow suicide. More angry now than afraid, Ethan went back upstairs.

TWO

Mannering had made a good dent on the bottle he was drinking and had, from somewhere, produced a second one for when he finished. His eyes were already glazed, and he was about to take another swig when Ethan snatched the bottle from his hands and threw it across the cabin.

"Hey, whathehellareyoudoing?" Mannering slurred.

"You lying son of a bitch. You've wasted all this time. All this time we could have been heading back, and you've had us sit here."

"Whaddyamean?"

"Fuel, Mannering. You said we were out, but the gauges say we have half a tank."

"So what?"

"So what? Why the hell are we just sitting here and letting that thing circle us? We could be out of here."

Mannering shook his head. "It won't work," he said, taking two attempts to try and unscrew the cap of the second bottle of whiskey. "I knowwhatimdoing."

Ethan reached for the bottle, but Mannering pulled it away from him. "Don't start with me."

Ethan went to the controls of the boat, scanning the instruments. "Where's the key? Where's the starter key?"

"Gone," Mannering slurred, finally gaining access to the bottle. "I threw it in the water."

"You didn't."

"Or maybe I've got them in my pocket. Who knows?"

"This isn't a game, we could die out here."

Mannering grinned and looked beyond Ethan through the window. "Hey, it's snowing."

Ethan glanced out of the window and saw that, as drunk as he was, Mannering was right. A light snow had started to fall, the flakes melting as they made contact with the window.

"Give me the keys, Mannering."

"Why don't you come and take em?" he replied, setting the bloody knife on the table in front of him.

Ethan crossed the room, fuelled by fear more than common sense. Mannering snatched up the knife, but Ethan wasn't interested in the blade. He wanted the bottle. He snatched it from the table and went out on deck with it, Mannering stumbling after him.

"You give me that back, that's mine, I brought that with me."

Ethan held it out over the side of the boat. "Keys first, then you can have it."

"Keys?" Mannering grunted, eyes wild as he fished in the filthy pockets of his jeans. "I'll give you the keys alright, you son of a bitch."

Mannering took the key chain out of his pocket, and like Ethan, held it over the side of the boat. "You ever played poker, boy?" Mannering said, his breath fogging in the cold air. "You ever gambled something where it was a must-win situation?"

Ethan was staring at the keys hanging over the side just as much as Mannering was staring at the bottle. "I'm prepared to take a chance."

"Are you really? Even though if I drop these keys we're both dead?"

"What if I drop the bottle? We both know you need this, Mannering. You're an alcoholic. I'd bet that right now, this bottle means more to you than anything."

"He begged, you know," Mannering said, an elastic grin

stretching across his cheeks. "He begged for mercy, begged me to help him even as I cut him up. Did I tell you I ate a bit of him? A bit of flesh?"

"Shut up."

"I wanted to try it, see. I wanted to see what it tasted like."

"Stop it, don't say those things."

"He could have lived, the bleeding had stopped, but I wanted to try it. I wanted to see if those stories about flesh eaters out in the wilderness were right. It' not bad, you know. It's a safer way to live, safer than coming out here and risking it all against those things."

"Then let's go back, you can go off into the wastelands and live that way, just let me go back to the village first."

"And let you live in the place I helped build? I was one of the first, I was one of the founders of that damn place!" Mannering spat. "You don't get to tell me anything. You think I can go back there, you think I want to go and face those people and tell them their beloved Barnes is dead, that he died on my watch?"

"It was an accident, I'll tell them what happened."

"Oh I bet you will, right after you tell them how I cut him up and ate some of him, how I attacked you, how I chased this fish all the way out here and got us stranded. They'll banish me, kick me out. I built that damn place." He was screaming now, and his grip on the keys was loose.

"We can work it out, Mannering. We can figure a way to put it right."

"Fuck you, who are you to talk to me? You turn up here then bully your way into coming out here, doing my job, the job I'm relied on to do. You're nothing, nobody. You don't matter."

Mannering sneered, lowering his voice. "Want to know a secret? I know why our fish won't leave us alone."

Ethan was stunned, unable to respond. Mannering went on.

"See, right after I knocked you out and tied you up, he came to investigate, got curious about why we were chasing him so far. He wouldn't come close to the boat, though, we had no bait, so I had to use Barnes. There was plenty of blood, plenty of fleshy bits to tempt him in. When he got close, I got him hooked, snagged his fluke on the winch."

Ethan glanced to the winch, noticing for the first time that the cable was in the water.

"He took a lot of line," Mannering went on. "Dragged us for a quarter of a mile before he got tired. I tried to drag him in, I turned us around to head for home and started to pull him in, but he pulled back and nobody went anywhere. See, we have us a stalemate. We can't pull him and he's too tired to pull us. We're stuck."

Ethan stared at the water, then back at Mannering.

"So you see it makes no difference if you have the keys or not. You can't go anywhere. That bastard is as stubborn as me, and neither of us are willing to budge."

"Then let it loose, let it go."

Mannering barked a shrill laugh which rolled away into the open ocean. "You think I haven't tried that? You think I would if I could? Winch controls are broken, burned out when I was trying to drag him. Even so, the hooks are in deep, he's really tangled. No way to free the big son of a bitch, so I decided we'd go out like men and die here on the boat with him."

"What if we kill it somehow?"

"That won't work," Mannering said, shaking his head. He was afraid, and couldn't hide it anymore. "You don't get this, do you? Why do you think those things don't just wash up on the shore? Why do you think we never see them floating around?"

Ethan shrugged. He didn't know.

"I'll tell you why. It's because they sink. Our big fish out there has to be fifty feet, maybe more. My guess is he weighs more than a hundred tons. What do you think will happen when he eventually tires and dies?"

"He sinks," Ethan said quietly

"He sinks," Mannering repeated. "And when he does, his hundred-ton carcass will go straight to the bottom and drag us down with it."

Ethan felt as if he had been punched in the gut.

"So when you ask why I'm not doing anything to stop us from dying, maybe, just maybe it's because, for all intents and purposes, we're already dead. We can't go anywhere, and we can't stay. In the old world, they would call that a conundrum. So you tell me, what do we do?"

"I...I don't know," Ethan said.

"Then stop acting like a dick and give me back my booze so I can at least die happy."

"No. You don't deserve to die happy, not after what you did to Barnes."

He acted on instinct, reared back and threw the bottle, watching it spin end over end, spilling its contents into the ocean before the bottle landed and sunk without trace.

"You son of a bitch!" Mannering grunted as he charged across the deck, tackling Ethan to the ground, knocking the wind out of him. Ethan grunted, trying to catch his breath, the pain in his shoulder exploding through him. He saw a flash of silver, then Mannering was stabbing at him with the knife his face twisted into a grimace. Ethan reacted on instinct, grabbing Mannering's hand, trying to deflect the frenzied attack. They were leaning on the transom, dangerously close to falling over the edge into the water. Ethan felt agonising pain in his arm as Mannering's knife hit home, slicing open the skin of his upper arm and sending hot blood cascading into the water.

The reaction was immediate, the wake came, rolling slowly towards them as the weakened beast beneath the waves honed in on the potential food source. Ethan squirmed underneath Mannering, who was watching the creature come closer, his face twisted into a grin.

"She's coming for you, boy. She's coming to take you."

"Please let me up," Ethan said, staring at the water.

The creature breached, cascading icy water into the air. It rolled to them on the surface, unseen appendages propelling it through the water.

"When it takes you, I'm going to see it, I'm going to see it up close. Look, he's watching you."

The creature had breached, its massive eye staring at them both as they struggled on the rear of the boat. Fresh cuts and scars criss-crossed its body where Mannering had attached it during the chase.

"When you see Barnes, tell him it wasn't personal," Mannering grunted, the booze on his rancid breath making Ethan feel nauseous.

The creature accelerated, speeding towards the boat. Ethan braced himself, wondering how it would feel, wondering how much awareness he would have as those immense, serrated teeth pulverised him into nothing. He closed his eyes, waiting for the pain to come.

Instead, he was thrown across the deck, slamming into the doorframe leading to the interior. The creature had struck the rear quarter of the boat, splintering the old wood with ease and rupturing the barely seaworthy steel hull, the boat split in two, each section drifting apart. Mannering was in the rear section by the winch, screaming as he gripped on to the winch cable, the broken end section already filling with water on its way to sinking Ethan was in the main bulk of the vessel, but even that was beyond saving. The entire rear section was missing, and water was thundering in by the gallon. Ethan stared, still on the ground, watching the separated transom make a slow rotation as it sank beneath the waves. Mannering jumped into the ocean and started to swim, head down, legs kicking as he headed towards Ethan. All around him, the boat was starting to creak as it lost its battle to stay afloat.

"Help me," Mannering screamed as he covered the short distance to Mannering. "Help me up, damn you,"

Ethan watched as Mannering grabbed at the splintered wood, fighting against the pull of the water as it rushed into the empty spaces below the water level.

"Pull me up, the water is too strong."

Ethan was barely listening. Behind Mannering, the creature had surfaced again, its scale impossible to comprehend, the power it possessed beyond question. It was watching them. Mannering was screaming now and losing his battle to avoid being sucked under into the exposed innards of the vessel by the force of the water.

He reached down and grabbed Mannering's arm and pulled him out of the water, his feet scrambling for purchase on the shattered deck.

"Thank you, thank you, I knew you were a good kid, I just knew it," Mannering said. Ethan grabbed him by the shoulders, locking eyes with Mannering.

"You deserve this," he whispered, then shoved with everything he had, sending Mannering back into the water. Mannering's screams were cut off as his head went beneath the waves.

Behind him, the creature moved, a single flick of its massive fluke closing the distance. Mannering resurfaced, opened his mouth as if to speak, and then was gone in an explosion of blood and bone as the creature took him. As it dived beneath the water, Ethan saw the winch cable wrapped around its fluke, the barbs digging in deep.

Silence.

The rear section of the boat had already disappeared beneath the waves and was now being dragged around unseen by the mammoth creature.

The remaining section of the boat on which Ethan stood was starting to dip towards the water as its insides filled with ocean. Water was already up to his ankles. He clambered up onto the roof of the wheelhouse, fighting against the gradient as the boat lost its battle to stay afloat. His hope that the creature would leave him alone now that it had Mannering were destroyed when he saw the wake come again, rolling against the natural ebb of the tide as it came to investigate. Ethan surveyed the debris field from the boat, which was now bobbing across the surface of the ocean. He saw blood, and for a moment, he was sure it was what was left of Mannering, before realising it was Barnes he was looking at. The tub which had contained him gone, his separate limbs bobbing along in the ocean, and in turn compelling the creature to investigate. It approached the carcass, breaching the water and skimming across the front edge of the vessel with its massive mouth agape, bloody chunks of Mannering still clinging to its massive teeth. It took Barnes' torso in one, crushing it with ease and swallowing it down.

The boat was now sinking rapidly, its battle to stay afloat lost. Ethan was now treading water. He couldn't swim and was sure he was about to drown. He clung to a floating section of wood from somewhere within the wreckage, grimacing as the icy water bit into his body. For a moment, he couldn't breathe, then gasped and kicked his legs, struggling to stay afloat. He watched as the boat disappeared beneath the waves, leaving only debris and its one sole survivor behind. Once again, there was silence. Ethan had never known such cold, he was already going numb, and even breathing was hard. His injured arm and shoulder spilled hot blood into the water, which in turn brought the huge predator in the water to investigate.

From so low in the water, the wake looked like a mountain of water racing towards him. Never had he known such fear, such absolute all-consuming fear as in that exact moment. He could see it, its massive frame visible as it came to take the food the ocean had offered. Ethan bore it no grudge. It was a creature of instinct, honed to feed and survive on whatever it could. He could only imagine how frustrated it had become as it had been chained to the boat by Mannering, unable to hunt, swim or feed. Ethan knew he was dead anyway; he would either drown or die of the cold if the creature didn't take him first, and at least that way would be quick. He braced for it, clinging on to the floating wreckage with fingertips that were rapidly growing numb. He had never known such fear. The water exploded in front of him. Sweeping away the flimsy wreckage that had been keeping him afloat. He was underwater, tumbling in the currents, wondering what had happened and why he wasn't dead. He opened his eyes, desperately kicking and thrashing for the surface which seemed so far away.

The creature that had been coming for him was there, or more accurately, half of it was. It had been completely severed in the middle, bitten in two by the other creature, which had slammed into its side. Even at fifty feet, the creature Mannering had been chasing was positively tiny compared to the beast Ethan could now see. It was at least three hundred feet in length, its body a twisted mass of flesh. Bone grew on the outside of the skin, and its side was lined with deformed flipper-like appendages. Milky eyes were scattered about its head and side, and its huge gaping mouth was filled with razor-sharp teeth, each as tall as he was. The creature turned, and in a single bite, engulfed the front half of the creature that just seconds ago was about to kill Ethan, taking the whole forward section is one bite, shaking its massive head as it chewed, and in turn, sending Ethan tumbling backwards. Something snagged him, a piece of wreckage from the boat. It pierced his stomach, sending a fresh torrent of blood into the ocean. The new giant of the ocean honed in on it instantly, moving towards Ethan. He had never seen anything so big, so impossibly huge. The diary Mannering had given him sprang to mind, the one about a similarly doomed fishing trip like this one that had ended in death. They were right, the ocean was no place for man, not anymore. It had become a hellish place filled with vile wonders beyond comprehension. All Ethan did know was that he didn't want to die on its terms; he would do it his own way. He would do it the same way as in the diary he had read. He opened his mouth and started to swallow the irradiated, foul water, coughing and choking and praying for death before the creature took him. As the world faded to darkness, Ethan was vaguely aware of a change in temperature as the giant beast slammed down its jaws on him. There was no pain, only silence and at least peace.

For Ethan, the nightmare was over.

CHECK OUT OTHER GREAT DEEP SEA THRILLERS

MEGA
by Jake Bible

There is something in the deep. Something large. Something hungry. Something prehistoric.
And Team Grendel must find it, fight it, and kill it.
Kinsey Thorne, the first female US Navy SEAL candidate has hit rock bottom. Having washed out of the Navy, she turned to every drink and drug she could get her hands on. Until her father and cousins, all ex-Navy SEALS themselves, offer her a way back into the life: as part of a private, elite combat Team being put together to find and hunt down an impossible monster in the Indian Ocean. Kinsey has a second chance, but can she live through it?

THE BLACK
by Paul E Cooley

Under 30,000 feet of water, the exploration rig Leaguer has discovered an oil field larger than Saudi Arabia, with oil so sweet and pure, nations would go to war for the rights to it. But as the team starts drilling exploration well after exploration well in their race to claim the sweet crude, a deep rumbling beneath the ocean floor shakes them all to their core. Something has been living in the oil and it's about to give birth to the greatest threat humanity has ever seen.

"The Black" is a techno/horror-thriller that puts the horror and action of movies such as Leviathan and The Thing right into readers' hands. Ocean exploration will never be the same."

CHECK OUT OTHER GREAT DEEP SEA THRILLERS

PREDATOR X
by C.J Waller

When deep level oil fracking uncovers a vast subterranean sea, a crack team of cavers and scientists are sent down to investigate. Upon their arrival, they disappear without a trace. A second team, including sedimentologist Dr Megan Stoker, are ordered to seek out Alpha Team and report back their findings. But Alpha team are nowhere to be found – instead, they are faced with something unexpected in the depths. Something ancient. Something huge. Something dangerous. Predator X

DEAD BAIT
by Tim Curran

A husband hell-bent on revenge hunts a Wereshark...A Russian mail order bride with a fishy secret...Crabs with a collective consciousness...A vampire who transforms into a Candiru...Zombie piranha...Bait that will have you crawling out of your skin and more. Drawing on horror, humor with a helping of dark fantasy and a touch of deviance, these 19 contemporary stories pay homage to the monsters that lurk in the murky waters of our imaginations. If you thought it was safe to go back in the water...Think Again!

CHECK OUT OTHER GREAT DEEP SEA THRILLERS

LAMPREYS
by **Alan Spencer**

A secret government tactical team is sent to perform a clean sweep of a private research installation. Horrible atrocities lurk within the abandoned corridors. Mutated sea creatures with insane killing abilities are waiting to suck the blood and meat from their prey.

Unemployed college professor Conrad Garfield is forced to assist and is soon separated from the team. Alone and afraid, Conrad must use his wits to battle mutated lampreys, infected scientists and go head-to-head with the biggest monstrosity of all.

Can Conrad survive, or will the deadly monsters suck the very life from his body?

DEEP DEVOTION
by **M.C. Norris**

Rising from the depths, a mind-bending monster unleashes a wave of terror across the American heartland. Kate Browning, a Kansas City EMT confronts her paralyzing fear of water when she traces the source of a deadly parasitic affliction to the Gulf of Mexico. Cooperating with a marine biologist, she travels to Florida in an effort to save the life of one very special patient, but the source of the epidemic happens to be the nest of a terrifying monster, one that last rose from the depths to annihilate the lost continent of Atlantis.

Leviathan, destroyer, devoted lifemate and parent, the abomination is not going to take the extermination of its brood well.

SEVEREDPRESS

f facebook.com/severedpress

twitter.com/severedpress

CHECK OUT OTHER GREAT
DEEP SEA THRILLERS

CHECK OUT OTHER GREAT DEEP SEA THRILLERS

SEA RAPTOR
by John J. Rust

From terrorist hunter to monster hunter! Jack Rastun was a decorated U.S. Army Ranger, until an unfortunate incident forced him out of the service. He is soon hired by the Foundation for Undocumented Biological Investigation and given a new mission, to search for cryptids, creatures whose existence has not been proven by mainstream science. Teaming up with the daring and beautiful wildlife photographer Karen Thatcher, they must stop a sea monster's deadly rampage along the Jersey Shore. But that's not the only danger Rastun faces. A group of murderous animal smugglers also want the creature. Rastun must utilize every skill learned from years of fighting, otherwise, his first mission for the FUBI might very well be his last.

OCEAN'S HAMMER
by D.J. Goodman

Something strange is happening in the Sea of Cortez. Whales are beaching for no apparent reason and the local hammerhead shark population, previously believed to be fished to extinction, has suddenly reappeared. Marine biologists Maria Quintero and Kevin Hoyt have come to investigate with a television producer in tow, hoping to get footage that will land them a reality TV show. The plan is to have a stand-off against a notorious illegal shark-fishing captain and then go home.

Things are not going according to plan.

There is something new in the waters of the Sea of Cortez. Something smart. Something huge. Something that has its own plans for Quintero and Hoyt.

 SEVERED**PRESS**

CHECK OUT OTHER GREAT DEEP SEA THRILLERS

MEGATOOTH
by Viktor Zarkov

When the death rate of sperm whales rises dramatically, a well-respected environmental activist puts together a ragtag team to hit the high seas to investigate the matter. They suspect that the deaths are due to poachers and they are all driven by a need for justice.

Elsewhere, an experimental government vessel is enhancing deep sea mining equipment. They see one of these dead whales up close and personal...and are fairly certain that it wasn't poachers that killed it.

Both of these teams are about to discover that poachers are the least of their worries. There is something hunting the whales...

Something big
Something prehistoric.
Something terrifying.
MEGATOOTH!

BLOOD CRUISE
by Jake Bible

Ben Clow's plans are set. Drop off kids, pick up girlfriend, head to the marina, and hop on best friend's cruiser for a weekend of fun at sea. But Ben's happy plans are about to be changed by a tentacled horror that lurks beneath the waves.

International crime lords! Deep cover black ops agents! A ravenous, bloodsucking monster! A storm of evil and danger conspire to turn Ben Clow's vacation from a fun ocean getaway into a nightmare of a Blood Cruise!

www.ingramcontent.com/pod-product-compliance
Lightning Source LLC
Chambersburg PA
CBHW051946170626
46808CB00007B/2504